I0669166

DOUBLE FAULT

By Sheila Claydon

Amazon Print 978-1-77362-750-2

Books We Love
A quality publisher of genre fiction.
Airdrie Alberta

Dedication and acknowledgements

With apologies to all the tennis players in my family....

Chapter One

Kerry scowled at the telephone. Why did it always ring when she was up to her elbows in flour? She brushed her hands together and wiped them across the front of her T-shirt.

"Hello."

"Kerry, can you stand in for me today? I've picked up some sort of stomach bug that's keeping me chained to the bathroom." Mel, joint owner of Melanie's Kitchen, the catering service she and Kerry were running on a shoestring, sounded worried.

Kerry's first reaction was one of amused disbelief. Workaholic Mel was never sick. She considered illness a self-indulgence that interfered with work and so didn't allow it into her life. Concern followed quickly, however, because if Mel was prepared to admit defeat then she must be feeling pretty rough.

"What are you taking for it?" she demanded, mentally reviewing the contents of her own bathroom cabinet in case she had something suitable.

"I've given up eating," her friend wasn't interested in discussing how best to treat her symptoms. "Look Kerry, can you manage or not? Mum says to tell you she'll collect the twins from the nursery, and Dad will bring the van and help at your end. It isn't a big spread. Just the cold buffet for forty you prepared yesterday, followed by coffee."

"Of course I can manage. Give me the details and then go back to bed," Kerry seized a stub of pencil and a notepad, resolutely ignoring the weariness that a week of broken nights had stamped on her face.

"You're a star!" She heard the relief in Mel's voice.

"I'm also your junior partner so I've enough clout to insist you stay put until you're completely better," Kerry reminded her drily.

"Save your mothering for the twins and concentrate. The lunch is scheduled for one o'clock at Greenleas Country Club."

"I didn't know it was open yet," Kerry said as she scribbled instructions.

"The pool and gym are being used but the hotel complex isn't finished yet. It opens sometime next month I think. The conference rooms are ready to go though, so the manager has agreed to let our client use them as long as he brings in outside caterers. I guess the fact he's running a big fitness drive for his executives helped. I expect the marketing people at Greenleas hope some of the conference delegates will be sufficiently inspired to join."

"So that's why fresh fruit and healthy options feature so prominently on the menu," Kerry glanced at the week's orders pinned to the notice board next to the telephone. Monday detailed a selection of cold meats, mixed salads, cheeses and seasonal fruit. It was very spartan by their normal buffet standards and it was already prepared and waiting in cooler containers in the hall.

Then, remembering what Mel had said about her father helping, she asked what time he would arrive.

"Ten minutes after you telephone him to say you're ready to leave and...oh no! Sorry Kerry...I've got to go. Now!"

Realizing she was listening to the dial tone, Kerry slotted the telephone back into its receiver while absentmindedly dusting off a floury handprint with the edge of her T-shirt. Poor Mel! Poor Kerry for that matter! This would happen during a week when the twins, fractious from colds, had kept her up half the night. Still, it was only nine-thirty, so she had plenty of time to organize her day before she had to make the short journey to Greenleas Country Club. She hurried back to the kitchen, washed her hands, and then plunged them back into the half mixed bowl of pastry.

Thirty minutes of concentrated work saw four cheese flans cooking in the oven and all the dirty bowls and dishes stacked in the sink. Kerry crossed the last of the items off Tuesday's list, wiped the flour from the counter, tossed the dishcloth onto the draining board, and returned to the telephone.

First she called the twin's nursery to explain her change of plan and ask someone to tell Ben and Lauren that Mary, Mel's mother, would collect them and take them back to her house. She smiled wryly as she did so, knowing they would be so excited by the prospect of a visit to the two people they loved best in the world next to Kerry, that they wouldn't give her a second thought. Then she telephoned Mel's parents.

Mary answered the first ring. "Kerry, I was just about to call you. George has to stand in as a volunteer driver for the hospital run because one of the other regulars hasn't turned up. He says to tell you he's really sorry but there's no one else."

"Not to worry. As long as you can collect the twins, I'll manage." Kerry forced herself to sound more confident than she felt about having to pile all the food into her own car and then lug it into the country club by herself.

"I'll leave here in plenty of time, and I'll walk them home through the park so they can feed the ducks. They'll enjoy that. Don't you worry about a thing. You know how I love to look after them."

"And they love visiting you," Kerry's smile carried across the wires to the woman at the other end of the telephone. "I honestly don't know what we'd do without you."

"You'd manage," Mary Parker hid her pleasure at Kerry's words behind a brisk reply but Kerry was thoughtful as she hung up because she wasn't at all sure she would manage without Mel and her parents.

Ever since the twins were tiny they had treated her like one of the family, including her in their Christmas and Easter celebrations, remembering birthdays, and always being available for babysitting. Mel teased her when she became sentimental about it, telling her the twins were the grandchildren she had no intention of providing herself, but Kerry knew she would never be able to repay the huge debt of gratitude she owed.

She continued to think about this as she tugged her T-shirt over her head, peeled off her jeans, and dropped them onto a bed that had seen more than its fair share of tears in the months following the twin's birth. She remembered those dreadful first weeks with a shudder; the endless feeds, the continual crying; her only support an overworked health visitor. She had gone for days without speaking to a soul, her heart shriveled with bitterness, her love for her babies threatened by a growing depression. Then she'd seen the advertisement for a junior partner/cook in a fledgling catering business and, realizing it was something she would be good at and which she could do from home, she had talked Mel into employing her. Ambitious, reliable, practical Mel had viewed the twins with dismay and started to say no. Then she had taken a second look at Kerry's set white face and given her the job.

Dismissing the painful memories with a frown, Kerry slipped her arms into a plain white blouse, zipped up her black skirt and then turned to the mirror to adjust her collar. The face that stared back at her was pale and tired with huge smoky-grey eyes and a tousle of chestnut colored hair. She pulled a face. White had never suited her. It made her look insipid.

In an effort to improve things she creamed her face and added blusher and a slick of pink lip-gloss. Her eyes, fringed with long curling lashes beneath a curve of dark brow, she left alone. Instead she used her hairbrush to good effect, smoothing her short hair into a gleaming cap as she brushed it behind her ears. Finally she added tiny gold earrings and stood back to view her reflection.

The blusher and lipstick went a long way towards camouflaging her tiredness and the earrings lent sophistication to a hairstyle that had been chosen for convenience rather than fashion. Only her hands let her down, the nails short and sensible, several of her fingers scarred with oven burns. She shrugged and turned away. It would have to do. If the client wanted glamour he would have to wait until Mel recovered.

* * *

Loading the car took longer than she'd anticipated because she had to remove the twin's car seats to make some space for the

10

food, and then she snagged her tights against one of the cooler boxes. By the time she had changed into a fresh pair and checked everything against her list it was almost eleven o'clock. She began to panic when she suddenly remembered there was a route diversion between her house and Greenleas Country Club because of road repairs. Mel had cut the call before she could ask about the kitchen arrangements at the venue too. Would she be on her own, or would there be extra help? Did Melanie's Kitchen have to supply everything or would china and cutlery be available?

She contemplated telephoning her friend but was reluctant to disturb her in case she was asleep. After a moment's deliberation, she pulled boxes of paper plates, plastic tumblers and cutlery out of an overflowing hall cupboard and piled some from each into an empty carton, adding paper napkins and several plastic trash bags as she headed towards the front door.

Her worst fears were realized and it was almost noon by the time she reached Greenleas. A huge pantechnicon blocked the car park, and the main reception area was full of packing cases, ladders and open toolboxes. There was no sign of a receptionist, nor of anyone else, so with no one to ask, and desperate, she abandoned her car outside the main entrance and began to unload.

A printed notice with a large red arrow pointed her in the direction of the conference annex and she soon found herself standing in the middle of a large dining area staring in dismay at the tables and chairs stacked around the walls. A lone boiler full of cold water waited forlornly on a side table near the door. With a shaky intake of breath she lowered her boxes to the floor. Mel must have agreed to set out the tables and chairs as well as provide the food, and now she had less than an hour to do everything.

She was on her sixth and final journey to the car when the heel of her shoe caught between two paving stones and wrenched right off. Left with no choice but to don a pair of old trainers she kept in the car, she hoped nobody would notice. If she hadn't been so desperately worried about letting Mel down she might have seen the funny side and gone in search of the regular staff to rustle up some sympathetic help. As it was, she couldn't think straight. All she could remember was Mel's delight when she landed the Greenleas contract, and here she was, ruining it.

At ten minutes past one she was still putting the finishing touches to the buffet and thanking her lucky stars the conference was running late, when someone burst into the room behind her and fired a fusillade of abuse.

"What the hell do you think you're playing at blocking the reception area? We have a service entrance for contractors and if it's not too much trouble I'd like you to move your car. Now!"

The sarcasm that lashed across the dining hall stopped Kerry in her tracks and drained the blood from her face until her eyes were two enormous holes in a dead white mask. For three years she had tried to forget that voice, the seductive Irish lilt that used to send shivers down her spine whenever it whispered in her ear. Her fingers became nerveless and her knees turned to jelly but she answered bravely, keeping her back turned, hoping against hope that the voice's owner would go away.

"I'm sorry. I arrived late because of a route diversion and when I got here a furniture truck was blocking the service road. I meant to move the car as soon as I finished unloading but there was so much to do I didn't have time. I'll go and park it right away."

"Make sure you do." She heard him push against the door ready to exit but her relief was short lived because, as he turned to go, the delegates began to drift into the hall still discussing the conference as they made their way towards the buffet.

She heard his hiss of irritation as he crossed the floor. "For heaven's sake! Are you coping with all this on your own or is there someone else who can take over before the car park grinds to a complete halt?"

"I'm on my own," she still had her back to him as she rifled through her purse looking for her keys. "I'll move my car as soon as I've finished serving."

"Not on my watch you won't," he held out his hand for her car keys. It was a large, brown hand with the strong fingers and muscular forearm she remembered only too well. "Give them to me and I'll move it. It's bad enough having the car park blocked without the caterer abandoning post too!"

Kerry half turned and dropped the keys into his outstretched palm, praying that her short hair and practical clothes would stop him looking any closer. After all why should the great Pierce Simon be interested in the domestic help? It wasn't exactly his style.

"Kerry!" The disbelief in his voice provoked the trace of a reluctant smile as, her prayers unanswered, she was finally forced to turn right around and face him.

"Hello Pierce. I didn't think you'd recognize me," she kept her voice cool, trying to ignore a sudden inner turmoil as her heart began to thud erratically against her ribs.

"Well you're certainly different," his startled blue glance took in everything from her strained expression to the shabby trainers on her feet. "What are you doing? Seeing how the other half lives?"

She flushed at the scorn in his voice. "As it happens I'm the junior partner in Melanie's Kitchen."

"Next stop the Ritz I suppose," his half smile took some of the sting out of his words as he nodded towards her shabby trainers. Surprisingly she felt a bubble of laughter begin deep inside her as he nudged her sense of the ridiculous in the same way he used to do when he was the centre of her life. Hastily she quashed it and moved forward to supervise the buffet, determined not to place the Greenleas contract in any further jeopardy, and equally determined not to let him back into her nicely mended heart. His hand on her shoulder made her jump.

"I'll see you later," this time the smile was frosted as he acknowledged her deliberate cold shoulder. "Ask the receptionist to call me when you want your keys."

She didn't answer him as she began to dispense slices of meat and polite small talk to the delegates clustered around the buffet, and after a moment he shrugged and walked away.

She watched him go, seeing irritation in his swift stride and in his curt acknowledgment of the few people who recognized him. She tried to concentrate on that, on the part of him she disliked, the part of Pierce Simon that demanded constant attention and immediate gratification. Instead a more basic memory called to her so instead she found herself feasting on the length of his legs, his slim hips, his golden brown skin and his trademark tangle of sun streaked hair.

"Was that Pierce Simon?" a woman with long blonde hair asked as she spooned couscous salad onto her plate.

Kerry nodded silently as she abandoned an attempt to top up empty juice glasses with trembling hands.

"I thought so. He's quite something isn't he? I must say I haven't enjoyed watching

Wimbledon so much since he dropped out of the tennis scene."

"That's because you go for the legs instead of the backhand," the man next to her in the queue teased.

"I never pretend to anything else," she retorted with a grin. "I wonder what he's doing here though? I would have expected California to be more his style."

Me too. Kerry took some surreptitious deep breaths as she listened, trying in vain to quell the rosy blush that had begun to suffuse her body as she reacted to the lingering fragrance of Pierce's aftershave.

"He owns Greenleas," a younger man who looked as if he started every day with a five-mile jog explained. "Well he owns the whole estate actually. I think he's having a house built somewhere in the grounds, and he has some grandiose plans for developing the country club once the initial renovations are complete."

"You mean you actually know him?" As the blonde woman's voice cut across the general remarks Kerry heard the familiar edge of excitement, the sexual frisson that Pierce's presence seemed to engender in every woman he met.

"Sort of. I work out in the gym a couple of times a week and he's often there too."

His words evoked a provocative memory. Pierce in the tightest of Lycra shorts and vest, his chest and arms glistening with sweat, his hair drenched into tight curls as he pushed himself to physical limits. She remembered the ripple of his muscles and the sinuous length of his legs as he dipped and twisted in an agony of exercise, and then later the shower, hot and relaxing. She could almost feel the water cascading across her back as he pulled her in with him, ignoring her protests and pushing aside the heavy, wet strands of her long straight hair to kiss her neck and to…

Abruptly she surfaced as someone asked her for a knife, and then busied herself preparing coffee while the conversation continued to ebb and flow around her. It was mainly speculation about Pierce's decision to leave the tennis circuit nearly two years earlier when he was still close to his peak.

Kerry listened, surprised at just how ignorant three years of struggling alone had made her. It had left no time for newspapers or magazines, no money for television, so that caught up in a daily round of dirty nappies and pureed carrot, she had missed his premature retirement. She had tried to distance herself of course, smashing her memories as viciously as he had once smashed tennis balls, so why should her main reaction be one of shock? After all it had to come one day, so why not before his fitness began to decline? By retiring early he'd escaped the ignominy of tired muscles and slower reactions as he faced ever younger opponents across the net.

"I wonder how old he is." The blonde woman was still musing about his other attributes.

"Thirty-three," the words were out before Kerry could stop herself and she blushed.

"You too!" The woman laughed. "Funny how that potent macho image gets to us all isn't it, even whilst we all insist we're fighting for equal rights. What else do you know about him?"

That he's six foot and three inches tall, was born in November, has an Irish mother and an English father, likes jazz and fast cars, kisses like a dream, thinks he's god's gift to women, and is the most arrogant self-obsessed member of the opposite sex you are ever likely to meet! The words buzzed round and round, unuttered, in Kerry's head as she gave a slight shrug and turned away. The woman would find out for herself soon enough anyway. From the way she was cross-questioning the young man who had claimed such a tenuous acquaintance with Pierce, she had every intention of following through. It was a syndrome Kerry knew well, and one that Pierce had never been averse to encouraging with a mild flirtation of his own.

* * *

By two-thirty Kerry was alone and she wrapped and stacked mechanically, tipping paper plates into two black trash bags and retrieving crumpled napkins and plastic cups from beneath tables and off windowsills. Finally everything was tidy and she knew she couldn't put off the evil moment any longer. She needed her car keys so she had to find and face Pierce.

Leaving the boxes and cooler containers near the door she made her way to Reception. The area was clear now and a girl with purple nails and a matching lipstick was sitting behind a large wooden desk.

"I…would you call Mr. Simon for me please," Kerry flushed with embarrassment as the receptionist looked her up and down and obviously found her wanting. "He has my car keys. My car was blocking the entrance," she added hastily, hoping this was enough to disassociate her from any personal connection in the girl's mind. Then she turned away and pretended to read the notices pinned to an adjacent board while the girl called Pierce's cell phone.

He came almost immediately, striding across the high gloss floor while he rapped out a stream of instructions to a young man in a tracksuit who was jogging to keep up with him.

"Finished?" He broke away from his companion and came across to where Kerry was trying to look interested in a poster about a Yoga class.

"Yes thank you," she held out her hand. "If you'll give me my keys and tell me where you've parked my car, I'll load it from the service entrance."

"And then I suppose you're going to push it home." Pierce made no attempt to hand over the keys as he stood looking down at her, his arms folded across a broad expanse of chest.

She frowned at his words, wishing she wasn't so affected by the tantalizing and far too familiar tang of his aftershave. "Of course not. Please give me my keys Pierce. I'm not in the mood for games."

"Nor am I!" Without warning he took her arm and ignoring her protests, propelled her at speed across the reception area to a door marked private. Pushing her inside he closed it firmly behind him and flipped the lock before waving her towards a dark blue leather couch.

"Now we are guaranteed some privacy, you can listen to me. Your car won't start. A mechanic is working on it at the moment so you're not going anywhere yet, which suits me fine because I think you owe me some sort of explanation and I am quite prepared to stay here until I get one."

Suddenly Kerry's legs wouldn't hold her and she folded onto the couch with an inward groan. It was all so unfair. She had always known she would have to face him again one day and she'd lived and relived this scene over and over again, except that in her imagination Pierce was the supplicant to her successful businesswoman. She'd always pictured herself elegantly dressed in a tailored suit and a designer blouse; in control of her emotions; cool and confident; prepared for the confrontation she knew was coming. She stared miserably at the scuffed trainers that made her slender legs look too thin and the smear of tomato relish on her white blouse. She might have known her dreams wouldn't come true. They never had as far as Pierce was concerned, which was why she had walked out on him three years ago when she was two months pregnant; too proud to ask for his help; too vulnerable to risk his contempt.

He took advantage of her silence to use his cell phone to order coffee. It gave Kerry the breathing space she needed. By the time he'd finished her chin was up and she was ready to protect herself and the twins from the one person who should have been the centre of their lives.

"Explanation?" Her smile was carefully positioned, one eyebrow raised quizzically.

"Yes, explanation dammit!" His brows drew together in a familiar scowl as he crossed the room to sit next to her. "While I'm on court playing one of the most important matches of my life you pack up your wardrobe and disappear. No warning. No explanation. Nothing. I was out of my mind with worry until I found your note. Why did you do it Kerry? What happened to make you run away?"

She managed a nonchalant shrug, hating what she was about to do but unable to think of an alternative. "I told you in the note. I was fed up with following you around the tennis circuit. Fed up with not having a life of my own."

"Well you sure as hell managed to hide your misery when you were buying up Paris and living the highlife in London and the States," he drew his brows together again in a disbelieving frown. "There has to be something else, or was it someone else."

She feigned a bored indifference as she met his puzzled blue gaze. "There was nothing…except I'd just had enough. All those hours of watching you play and then listening to you dissect your game…it was boring Pierce. So was only being able to socialize with other tennis players. I wanted more but you never listened to me. Not properly. It was always 'we'll talk about it later Kerry, after the next tournament'. In the end I'd had enough and besides, after nearly a year together, I wanted to leave good memories behind. If I'd told you I was going and why, there would have been arguments and bitterness."

That bit at least was true she told herself, hoping against hope he would buy her story and lose interest. After all he'd only ever had to click his fingers for a bevy of beauties to come running, so why should he bother about an old flame who'd walked out on him three years ago, particularly one who had lost her looks and her fortune.

"Memories! I wanted more than memories Kerry, and I thought you did too. I thought we had a future together." His voice bit into her thoughts as he leaned forward and grasped her wrist.

She dredged up every ounce of scorn she had in her and looked him squarely in the face, not flinching at his expression, ignoring the compelling draw of the deep blue eyes that had melted her so often in the past. "Don't be ridiculous Pierce. A future is only possible in the real world, away from constant travel and a different hotel room every week. You never once asked me what I wanted in all the time we were together. You never even wondered how I filled my time while you trained and practiced for hours and hours each day. You never considered I might be bored. You never thought about the future except in terms of matches and tournaments. You just liked having some arm candy to fill in the gaps and add color to your publicity. I was just a pretty face on the terraces for the television cameras to pick out while you changed ends."

He stared at her. "Is that what you really think or is it some sort of excuse?"

Before she could answer there was a tap on the door. Standing up abruptly, Pierce answered it. A girl in a pink overall carried in a tray with mugs, a coffee jug and cream set out neatly on a white cloth. At a growl from Pierce she placed it on the corner of the desk and then, with an anxious glance in his direction, scurried from the room. Kerry forced a light laugh.

"Still as gracious as ever I see. Haven't you learned yet that an occasional thank you takes you a long way?"

For a moment she thought she had gone too far as the dark wings of his eyebrows drew together, but then he laughed. It was a sharp, humorless sound and his smile didn't reach the cool blue of his eyes, but it deflected the tension between them.

He poured coffee into the two mugs. "Well! Well! You've changed in more than appearance haven't you? Obviously the tennis circuit stifled the real Kerry Farrow. I had no idea your ditsy image was a cover up for the professional woman straining to get out."

She winced; knowing how ridiculous she must seem but determined to make him believe tennis had driven her away. Pierce's memories were of a slender twenty-year-old with long straight hair that hung like a silk curtain halfway down her back. A girl whose almond shaped nails were always polished and who only ever wore designer clothes, from the jeans stretched to the limit across an impudent butt, to the full-on glamour of a Versace evening dress. In those days even her belt would have cost twice as much as the whole outfit she was wearing now. She felt a momentary stab of self-pity as she smoothed the front of her cheap chain store skirt. It prompted an angry answer.

"Well at least this Kerry Farrow is more productive than the sort of accessory you demanded. There are more important things in life than boosting the male ego."

"A sharp tongue too, but it wasn't all bad was it? I seem to remember we had one or two

24

mutual interests. " He drained his mug and replaced it on the tray. Then he walked across the room and pulled her to her feet. "Remember this?"

She saw the kiss coming and tried to turn her head, drooping her eyelids against the heady nearness of his body, trying not to drown in the familiar musky scent of his skin. He laughed aloud, his teeth gleaming white against the golden tan of his face, and then his lips were pinned to hers, his tongue honey-sweet as it probed the moisture of her mouth.

She resisted, her teeth clenched together, her palms pressing hard against the muscled smoothness of his chest, but he merely shifted position, unbalancing her, so that her fiercely resistant hands clutched instinctively at his shirt. Then he pulled back slightly and looked deep into her eyes before his lips began to move provocatively across her mouth and undid all her resolve. And as she began to respond, her arms sliding inexorably upwards towards the curls at the nape of his neck, her back arching as he pulled her closer, his taunting laughter was slowly replaced by something else, something so familiar that their three years apart might never have been. She felt it in the taut strength of his arms and the racing tattoo of his heart as it pounded against her breast.

For a moment she was powerless against the force of a treacherous body that was welcoming him back with a need that set each nerve on fire as his caressing fingers pressed long forgotten triggers of desire. Then, with a cry of horror, she broke free, pulling away from his arms so violently he was taken unaware and let her go. They faced one another, flushed and frustrated.

"So you haven't forgotten. Paper plates and napkins haven't quite taken over your life then Kerry," Pierce was almost contemplative as he spoke, holding himself in check as she walked unsteadily towards the door.

"No more than tennis took over yours," she aimed her punches low, wanting to upset him, ready to do and say anything that would help her to forget how she had felt when he kissed her. She willed herself to remember why she had walked out on him.

"Tennis is not my life any more," he spoke slowly and deliberately. "I'm more than a travelling ball machine now Kerry. I've a home and a business that allows me to work more or less regular hours. All that's missing is the girl."

She turned to face him then, her eyes huge with pain despite the whiplash of her tongue. "A commodity that was never in short supply as I remember it, so I won't wish you luck."

"You don't need to. Your luck always travels with me," he fingered a chain at his throat, pulling a small medallion up through the open neck of his polo shirt.

A small topaz set in gold winked across at her, reminding her of the day she had bought it in a small village high in the mountains of Italy. She'd noticed it when they were window-shopping because it was engraved with a small scorpion, and Pierce had laughed when she told him it was his birthstone. Then she'd dragged him into the shop and bought it with the last of her money, not knowing that within weeks her father would stop her allowance.

He had been unaccountably touched when she fastened it around his neck. He had pulled her close and held her so tightly she had protested. Afterwards he'd always worn it, saying it brought him luck.

Kerry gave him a bitter look as she remembered the memento he had given her on that same stolen holiday. It had been one of those halcyon times that had occurred far too infrequently in their relationship. With Pierce between tournaments they had managed to leave the tennis world behind them for a few days to grab a short time alone in a tiny secluded bungalow surrounded by olive groves. It had been a magical time as they lazed by their own private pool and played house for seven glorious days, shutting out the pressurized world of a sport that would soon reclaim him. It had also been the time that immature, scatterbrained Kerry Farrow had forgotten to take her contraceptive pills. What an irresponsible child she had been.

"I didn't realize you were so sentimental," she stamped on her memories with vitriol. "I thought you would have discarded it years ago. After all it's not worth much."

"That's where you're wrong," Pierce caught her hand as she reached again for the door, his eyes an unfathomable navy blue. "It's worth a great deal to me."

Chapter Two

His hand on her arm evoked too many memories and churned up already disturbed emotions. Hastily she moved away.

"Stop playing with me Pierce and give me my car keys." She didn't believe the lucky charm routine for a moment. He was just piqued by her attitude. She'd seen him in action far too often to believe the intent look and velvet phrase meant a thing. It was a purely reflex reaction, a matter of pride that nobody should leave his presence without succumbing to the well-known Simon charm. She had seen him indulge it all over the world, seen hardened television journalists melt at his smile, seen female fans wait for hours for his autograph. She had even fallen for it herself and how! But that was all behind her now and all she wanted to do was to get away from him and go back to the life she was beginning to make for herself.

"I told you, your car won't start," he answered her as if she were a particularly annoying child as he let his hand drop to his side. "Anyway what's the hurry? The least you can do is stay and have dinner with me and tell me what it is that you've been doing since we were together."

Their eyes met, his blue and calculating, hers grey and stormy. She knew what he was thinking; that in two or three hours he could win her round and put her back into his bed for as long as he wanted her. A tiny thread of warning sounded in her subconscious telling her he was probably right, but it didn't matter because she wasn't going to give him the chance to find out. She wasn't going to make the same mistake twice.

"No thank you," her refusal was formal and polite. "I haven't finished work for the day and I'm busy this evening."

"Tomorrow then?" His expression sharpened as he searched her face, trying to decipher her reluctance.

"Sorry," she gritted her teeth as she attempted a disinterested shrug. "The fact is I'm pretty tied up these days what with one thing and another."

And that isn't a lie she told herself as she gave him an unblinking stare. What with looking after the twins and cooking for Melanie's Kitchen she hadn't a spare minute to call her own. From the moment Ben and Lauren woke her at six every morning, to the time her head hit the pillow around midnight, she rarely stopped working. She fitted shopping and cooking into their nursery and nap times as much as possible, saving the inevitable housework and laundry until they were in bed in the evening. It meant she was often on the go for eighteen hours with hardly a break, and if the twins were ill, as they had been this past week with fretful colds, then her five or six hours of precious sleep dwindled alarmingly, leaving her pale and hollow eyed. She knew she was too thin as well, so that most of her clothes hung on her and did little to enhance any remaining curves. In fact she couldn't think of one single reason for Pierce to pursue her, and after glaring at her for several seconds, he apparently felt the same.

"In that case let's see if the mechanic has finished with your car," anger choked his voice as he held open the door and waited for her to precede him.

They didn't speak as they crossed the car park under a roiling mass of rain clouds. The mechanic working on her car stood up as they reached him and began to pack away his tools. She gave a sigh of relief. At least it was mended, so now she could ask for a bill she probably couldn't afford, and leave. Her hopes were short-lived however, because when he saw her, the man gave an apologetic shrug.

"The head gasket's a goner. I'll have to tow it back to the garage."

Kerry's heart plummeted. It sounded expensive, far too expensive for her meager resources if she and the twins were to eat well until the end of the month.

"Are you sure? I mean couldn't it be something...a bit...smaller?" She hurried forward and peered into the intricacies of the open bonnet.

"Cheaper you mean," he chuckled as he wiped his hands on a strip of oily rag. "Afraid not. And your tires are near the legal limit too. You need to trade this one in and start again."

"But I've only had it for a few months. The man who sold it to me said it was extremely reliable with years of wear in it," Kerry wailed, forgetting about Pierce as she concentrated on her car. How on earth was she going to manage without transport and how was she going to pay for a new head gasket.

"A private sale," the mechanic shook his head sorrowfully. "You've been taken for a ride sweetheart. I see it all the time. Now do you want me to patch it up or don't you?"

"I suppose you'll have to," she sighed, searching in her bag for a scrap of paper. "Here's my name and telephone number. Let me know when it's ready to be collected."

He pocketed her hastily scribbled details with a nod and then started whistling as he unhitched the rope from his tow truck. The shrill noise grated on Kerry. He had no right to sound so happy when her world was collapsing around her. That car had taken everything she had left in the bank and it was her one material donation to Melanie's Kitchen. Mel had provided everything else from the initial financial outlay to a new van with a company logo to impress clients. All Kerry had done was buy an old estate car to cope with the bulk shopping and to transport prepared food to Mel's apartment when her friend didn't have time to collect it. That and her cooking skills were all she had to offer while on the debit side she had the twins constantly demanding her attention, interrupting phone calls, even spoiling food left on the kitchen counter if she turned her back for a moment.

"You look frozen," Pierce's voice, close to her ear, brought her attention back to the cold wind whipping across the tarmac and for the first time she realized she was shivering.

"I am," she acknowledged the damp winter weather with a grimace. "This blouse was not designed with windy car parks in mind."

The expression in Pierce's eyes as he looked down at her reminded her that her blouse was not really designed at all. Instead it resembled something particularly unattractive that might have been left over from her school days. She raised her chin. He could think what he liked. Designer labels cost money better spent on car repairs. She pulled out her cell phone, hoping there was enough credit left to call Mel's father.

"I'll wait in reception while I arrange for someone to collect me and all the boxes." She hoped desperately that George had finished his Good Samaritan act by now so she wouldn't have to order a taxi.

"Don't be any more of a damn fool than you can help Kerry," Pierce's over-tested patience finally gave way as they retraced their steps across the car park. "I'll take you home or back to your work base, whichever you want, assuming you can bear to stay in my company for another hour or so."

"But that's ridiculous," she forced herself to ignore his sarcastic reference to her bolting act three years ago. "There's no need for you do that when I can easily ask a friend to help?"

He pushed open the door and motioned her inside. "I'm not doing it out of the kindness of my heart. I'm doing it because I'm curious. Curious about whatever took you away from me at such speed three years ago. And curious about whatever it is that's got you behaving like a cat on hot bricks every time you look at me."

* * *

They loaded his car in total silence. The incongruity of the cardboard boxes and plastic coolers against the plush interior of his shiny black Mercedes was lost on Kerry as she worried about what would happen when they reached her house. If she could have gotten away with it, she would have directed him to Mel's, but somehow it didn't seem fair to involve her friend. Besides, it would mean an explanation and she had an uncomfortable feeling Mel might disapprove if she knew the twin's father was being kept in total ignorance of his children. Not that Kerry had ever meant to deceive her but, somehow, Mel and her parents had assumed Kerry had been abandoned by an irresponsible boyfriend when he found out she was pregnant, and it had been easier to leave it like that. No! They mustn't learn about her past relationship with Pierce or they might put two and two together before she was ready to tell him about the twins. She would just have to let him drive her home and brazen it out.

"Where's your coat?" Pierce slid the last two boxes into place and straightened up, pulling on a padded jacket against the wind.

"I left it in my car," she shook her head impatiently. "It really doesn't matter."

He ignored her as he dragged a soft blue cashmere sweater from beneath the clutter that now filled his car. "Put this on before you freeze to death."

Her protest died unuttered as she saw the determined expression in his eyes and she pulled it over her head. It smelt of him, a familiar, warm, musky smell that enveloped her as she climbed into the passenger seat, and made her hands tremble when she attempted to fasten her seat belt. It was too evocative; the memories it unleashed were too painful. How was she going to bear it?

Silently Pierce leaned across and fastened the belt for her, his hands brushing against her fingers. She looked away, hoping he would put her clumsiness down to the cold, and studied the outline of Greenleas.

It was an impressive red brick building with a wide terrace to one side screened by specimen plants and shrubs. There were several tennis courts to the rear and, behind them, a putting green. In the summer it would be lovely, built as it was on the site of an old country house so that the surrounding trees were mature and the grass lush and green. The almost completed accommodation block was cleverly unobtrusive as it was constructed of the same red brick and joined to the main building by a glassed-in pergola that was thick with exotic flowers.

"What made you give up tennis and buy a country club?" Her question was abrupt as she voiced what had been on her mind since lunchtime. She couldn't fathom why the great Pierce Simon, darling of the centre court, would want to bury himself so far away from the action.

"This and that," he gave a slight shrug. "I doubt you would understand even if I explained."

Something in his cool response reminded her of the way he'd always distanced himself from her emotionally before a tennis match. It was something that had always left her feeling insecure and alone. Unconsciously she reacted as she had always done in the past. She tightened her lips and retreated into a taut silence that took them to the end of her road. Pierce didn't appear to notice anything amiss and he didn't speak again until he needed directions.

"What number?" He glanced across at her.

"Eighty-six," her answer was reluctant even though she knew she had no alternative. "It's halfway along on the right, just past the garage."

He drove slowly, eventually pulling into the curb outside her house into a space between a very battered Toyota and an old Rover with a crack across one window.

"I now understand about your car," his teeth gleamed briefly in the afternoon gloom. "You obviously bought it to keep up with the neighbors."

Kerry was suddenly very angry. How dare he sit there in his brand new Mercedes with its personalized number plate and poke fun at her neighbors, most of whom had to struggle to make ends meet. Forgetting that the Kerry Farrow he had known three years ago had had more money than sense, she glared at him, her eyes the same color as the wintry sky.

"I bought it because it was all I could afford. Most of us don't earn your sort of money Pierce. We barely earn enough to keep a roof over our heads let alone run a car. I bought four wheels and hoped it would hold together long enough for me to build my business. It didn't so I hope you're satisfied!"

She pushed open the car door as she finished speaking and stormed up the path, searching furiously through her purse for the front door key. By the time Pierce joined her carrying a box under each arm, she was turning it upside down for the third time.

"Oh no! I can't get in," her anger drained away as she remembered her door key was on the same ring as her car keys.

Surprisingly Pierce grinned as he lowered the boxes carefully to the ground. "I don't remember you being this disorganized in the past. Does that have something to do with your new working class image as well?"

"You…you arrogant…" words failed her as her fury came back in force. "What have you become Pierce? A social snob?"

"Now that is one thing I'm never likely to be," he folded his arms and leaned against the wall, apparently not at all bothered by her predicament. "This is my background, remember, and it took me a lot of years and hard work to climb out of it. Nobody gave me my car Kerry. I bought it with my own money and I've every intention of enjoying it, but it doesn't mean I've forgotten what it's like to be poor. I'm not going to lose respect for someone who can only afford to run a twelve-year-old car any more than I'm going to judge someone who can't afford to run one at all. No! The people I lose respect for are the ones who hide their own backgrounds and get a kick out of slumming it. Gives you a good feeling does it, to know you can play Cinderella until you get bored and then run back to Daddy?"

So that was what was bugging him. He thought she was playing at trying on someone else's lifestyle for a few months before retreating back into luxury. How stupid of her not to realize. If she had then she could have concocted some sort of story to throw him off track in the same way she had told him tennis bored her, when actually it was the part of him she had loved the most. She'd loved his tenacity and determination and had listened, fascinated, to the never-ending dissection of his every stroke. She'd watched his matches with baited breath, willing him to win, loving it when he did and ready for his frustration when he didn't.

Now she needed to do it all over again except it was too late. The trouble was she had lived with the truth for so long she had almost forgotten her former life. To her there was nothing odd about wealthy, extravagant Kerry Farrow living in a shabby house in a dilapidated terrace, but to Pierce it was a new experience. She wondered how to answer him. How much of the actual truth she could reveal without mentioning the twins because although she knew she had to tell him about them eventually, she wasn't ready yet.

"I...it's not...I can't go back...you see..." she stumbled and faltered as she tried to find the right words to explain that she no longer saw her father.

"You mean he threw you out of the house and stopped your allowance... but why would he do a thing like that?" The look of scorn on Pierce's face changed to bewilderment as he picked his way through her hesitant explanation.

She shrugged, her throat too full of bitterness to answer him. She had expected her father to be angry about her pregnancy of course. She had even expected him to demand an abortion. What she hadn't expected was that he would disown her so completely. It was something she could never forgive.

Even now she could hear the vitriol in his voice as he pronounced his judgment and then larded it with the final heartbreak. 'When your mother told me she was pregnant I wanted her to have an abortion but she wouldn't. She was obstinate, like you. Having you ruined our marriage Kerry. Children always do. Before you came along your mother was happy with me, with the life we were building together, but once you were born things changed. She didn't like leaving you, didn't like it when I insisted we holiday without you, and when I sent you off to boarding school she actually threatened to leave me. I soon put a stop to that, of course, but she was never the same again…and for that I blame you, the same as I blame you for her death. The cancer that started in her womb was your fault. You killed her Kerry!'

His words had torn her apart and for a short time she had even believed them. Then the memory of the day her mother first told her she was ill came back to her. The love in her eyes as she said the words that were to change Kerry's life forever was something she had never forgotten. Nor had she forgotten what she said after she told her about the cancer. 'You are the best thing that ever happened to me and I'd give anything to stay around until you grow up, but I can't my darling. This illness is going to get me first, so you're going to have to learn to fight your own battles sooner than I wanted you to."

They had hugged one another for a long time after that, only drawing apart when fourteen-year-old Kerry had finally accepted what her mother was telling her. Later, mingled with the tears, there had been practical discussions about school and about how things would be at home once her mother was no longer there. 'Your father will take it badly...he might even say and do things that will upset you. If he does then don't take it to heart. Whatever he tells you, just keep remembering it's not your fault. Nothing is your fault. Not this...not the problems between your father and me...I always wanted you Kerry...always.'

She hadn't really understood what her mother was trying to tell her until her father simply stopped speaking to her. It was immediately after a funeral where there had been no affection or sharing of grief, just an expectation she would keep her emotions in check as she greeted the other mourners. As soon as it was over he withdrew so completely that Kerry had to get herself back to her boarding school, and when she came home again he was still the same.

Although he had never been an easy father, far too wrapped up in his own life and career to ever be there with stories and cuddles, and far too much of a disciplinarian for her to ever be at ease in his company, he had at least

41

acknowledged her while her mother was alive. Now he simply ignored her, waving her away impatiently whenever she tried to speak to him. The only thing that didn't change was his financial support. As the owner of a highly lucrative investment company he was a very wealthy man with a strong media presence, and she soon learned that her monthly allowance had nothing to do with her and everything to do with the clothes and lifestyle that reflected his position in society. In the weeks immediately following her mother's death she often got it wrong. A messy hairstyle, a dress of the wrong length, not behaving appropriately when visitors came to the house, all resulted in a cruel tongue-lashing. Eventually she learned what was expected of her however, and with no other option, obeyed the rules he imposed.

Then, on her eighteenth birthday, everything changed. Calling her into his study he told her there was a job for her at Farrow Holdings. Plucking up every ounce of courage she had, she protested. When he discovered she wanted to train to be a hotel manager, his fury as he told her to forget it drained the color from his face. 'No daughter of mine is going to work as a skivvy in a hotel. You'll leave school right now and start working for Farrow Holdings immediately. It might knock some common sense into you as well as broaden your experience of the world.'

Well it had certainly done that all right, but not in the way he had anticipated. Instead she'd made a mess of the job she hated, and made a mess of her life as well. She sighed as she wondered why it had taken her so long to pluck up the courage to defy him. She had spent years making plans to leave home but had always been too frightened to follow any of them through. It had taken Pierce to rescue her. And look where that had got her.

All this flashed through her mind as Pierce watched her and she looked away in case he saw the truth in her eyes. She kept as close to the facts as she could. "We fell out about my lifestyle. He didn't like what I was doing with my life and when he realized I wasn't going to back down, he…we went our separate ways."

He thrust his hands into the pockets of his coat. "Well at least that explains why my letters went unanswered and why he refused to see me when I called. At the time I thought it was your doing and I was beyond angry."

Kerry's eyes widened in panic because it had never occurred to her that Pierce would try to track her down. She had assumed he would accept her letter of explanation at face value and quickly replace her with one of the many girls on the circuit.

"You didn't ever meet him then?" She heard the tremor in her voice.

"No! He all but had me kicked off his property. It was a most unpleasant experience and I've spent the past three years blaming you." Pierce's expression was grim as he pulled a bunch of keys out of his pocket and after a moment's deliberation, fitted the largest one into the keyhole.

Kerry watched him, her thoughts divided between the fact that he couldn't possibly know about her pregnancy if he hadn't managed to speak to her father, and the evidence that he was unlocking her front door.

The door won out. "Those are my keys," she stepped forward indignantly and snatched them out of his hands.

"Of course they are. I was hardly likely to leave all your keys over with a complete stranger was I?" She read smug satisfaction in his smile as he bent to retrieve the boxes and then nudged the door wider with his hip, leaving her with little alternative but to return to the car and start unloading the rest of her paraphernalia. Feeling like all sorts of an idiot she was still heaving them onto the pavement when he returned and gave a hiss of irritation.

"For god's sake go indoors and get warm. Make some coffee or something while I bring the rest of these in."

She swallowed the protest she was about to make and instead, realizing it would give her time to hide anything belonging to the twins, hurried ahead of him down the path. The hall was still strewn with cardboard boxes from her frantic foray into the cupboard earlier that morning and the sink was full of dirty dishes but, unusually, the children's toys were remarkably absent. They were still jumbled into a plastic tub in the tiny utility area off the

44

kitchen, next to their shiny wellington boots. Even their cereal bowls, bright with nursery rhyme characters, were hidden by piled up crockery. She gave a sigh of relief and concentrated on unpacking the cooler boxes as Pierce dumped them on the table, avoiding his eyes in case he looked sorry for her.

It was all very well for him to say he had come from this sort of background but it would take a lot to convince her he could truly remember what it was like. He had earned too much money for too long to look at her shabby little house with any sort of sentimentality. He would see it for exactly what it was; a home tacked together with second-hand furniture and other people's cast offs, and judge her accordingly.

As if in confirmation of her dark thoughts, he dumped the final two boxes on the table and then pulled out a kitchen chair and sat down. When he eventually spoke he sounded puzzled. "Can't you do better than this Kerry? Surely, with your education and background, you could have found something a bit more glamorous than working for a home catering service. I would have expected you to go for something that pays a bit better as well because it's obvious you're really struggling."

"I happen to enjoy it," she snapped, hastily closing a cupboard door on several tubes of brightly colored sweets and two lollipops. "And although it's none of your business, my education was very decidedly against girls having careers. Ambition was a dirty word at the school my father chose for me. It was a school noted for producing society hostesses with a good line in small talk and a limited repertoire of cordon bleu recipes, not somewhere that turned out doctors and lawyers."

"Come on, it can't have been that bad," he shook his head disbelievingly. "I don't remember you suffering from any glaring educational inadequacies. In fact I was always amazed by how many books you read while I was practicing."

"Well it was that or die of boredom," she surprised herself by smiling. "I guess I do owe something to the tennis circuit after all. It gave me a chance to educate myself."

"Am I supposed to be glad you don't hold it in total contempt?" Pierce's voice sharpened as he stood up. "Was that the only good thing about it Kerry? Was it only me who was happy during the months we were together because, if so, you're wasting your talents? You should be an actress."

"I didn't say I wasn't happy, only that I was bored sometimes," she flushed as she wove further lies into her story. "You were always so busy; there were so many demands on your time; so I guess it wasn't surprising I got fed up occasionally. After all there were limits to the number of saunas I could take, or the number of hours I could lie in the sun."

"…and the amount of money you could spend," his lips tightened as he referred to the mammoth shopping sprees she'd indulged in, treating herself at her father's expense until even Pierce had shouted at her. It was one of the few things they'd argued about; Kerry protesting it was only money while he retorted that it was obvious she'd always had it if she could spend it so irresponsibly.

Well things were certainly different now. She doubted she would ever be able to spend freely again, not even if Melanie's Kitchen fulfilled its ambition and became a financial success. She had learned a bitter lesson during the past three years, a lesson she was unlikely to forget although she wasn't about to admit it to Pierce.

"Oh that," she dismissed his remark with a shrug as she turned away and filled the kettle. "The money was there to spend wasn't it?"

"Until your father threw you out," he crossed the kitchen in three strides and stood in front of her, a troubled expression on his face. "Was it my fault Kerry? Was travelling with me the lifestyle he objected to? Would he have been happier about it if I'd bought you an engagement ring, made a commitment?"

"Probably," she busied herself with mugs and milk so she didn't have to look at him. "But it never came into it did it? Neither of us wanted any sort of commitment. I was too young and you were married to your career. Besides, in this day and age who cares about such things?"

"Apparently your father does," his hands on her shoulders made her jump and then wince as his fingers bit into her flesh.

"Put those mugs down dammit and look at me. If I was the reason you fell out with your father then I want to know about it. Stop putting up this ridiculous barrier and tell me what really happened."

She was saved by the telephone. It was Mel.

"Kerry, was everything okay today?"

"Fine," the lie rolled off her tongue with practiced ease. "How are you feeling now?"

"Back in the land of the living. Thanks for standing in for me."

"You're welcome. Do I need to cover for you tomorrow too?"

"Yes please. According to food hygiene regulations I have to be clear for at least forty-eight hours before I can start handling food again."

"In that case I'll do Wednesday as well," Trying to ignore the fact that Pierce was still standing too close to her, Kerry reached for her pad. "Give me the details and…oh no…my car is out of action. It broke down this afternoon."

"Don't worry. You can have the van. You can pick it up when Dad collects you. That's the other reason I phoned. He's on his way over to you. He feels so badly about letting you down at lunchtime that he's taking you home for tea."

"He doesn't have to do that," Kerry protested, panic building as she wondered how

48

she was going to get Pierce out of the house before Mel's Dad arrived and started talking about the children.

"Not my fight I'm afraid," she could tell Mel was grinning. "He just popped in here to see if I'd survived the day. As he was leaving he asked me to let you know he was on his way to give you time to gather up the twin's pajamas and whatever else they need for bedtime. Mum wants to send them home ready for bed. You know how she's always looking for an excuse to get them into the bath!"

Kerry sighed. This was a regular ritual and one she usually enjoyed because it gave her a break from the continual demands her children put on her, as well as providing Mel's mother with half-an-hour of pleasure as she soaped and powdered them. Tonight though, it was the last thing she wanted. For a start she wasn't sure if she could get rid of Pierce quickly enough and also she needed some thinking time, alone.

Now he'd found her again it was obvious he wasn't going to go away until he'd got to the bottom of her story, so she needed to decide what to do. She knew she should tell him about the children before things got out of hand but the thought frightened her far more than she would have thought possible. How would he react when he realized how much she had deceived him? That she had done it for all the right reasons didn't seem to matter now he was standing in front of her with a black frown on his face.

"Are you okay Kerry? Are you sure you can cope until Wednesday?" Mel's worried voice broke the silence.

"Of course I can. I was just finding a blank page on my pad," Kerry reached for a pencil and hoped Pierce hadn't noticed she had a totally clean sheet of paper in front of her.

* * *

The doorbell rang as she was scribbling down the last few details but although she hung up abruptly, barely giving Mel time to say goodbye, she was too late. Pierce had already taken the few steps necessary to cross her cramped hallway and open the door, and when she hurried through from the kitchen he was staring in total disbelief at the burly figure of Mel's father, George, who was sporting a very grubby twin on either arm.

Chapter Three

Lauren took one look at Pierce and burst into tears. She held her arms out to Kerry, her tiny body wracked by sobs of fright.

"Now, now! Mummy will think you haven't enjoyed yourself if you cry like that. Tell her what we did this afternoon," George tried to console her as he handed her over.

But Lauren wasn't listening as she clung to Kerry and buried her face in her neck. "No like," she sobbed. "Go 'way!"

Ben, however, was made of sterner stuff. "We bin Mel's," he told Pierce.

"You didn't go in though did you," George put in hastily. "You waved from the car so you wouldn't catch her old tummy bug, didn't you?" He was becoming more and more ruffled by Pierce's silent stare, and consequently more and more hearty.

"Wiv choclit," Ben agreed, swiveling his eyes round to give his mother a beatific smile.

"So I see," Kerry used a shaky hand to wipe away the smear of chocolate that ringed his mouth. "Was it good?"

But Ben had already dismissed his long finished chocolate bar and was trying to wriggle out of George's grasp. Always a child of the moment, he was more interested in Pierce.

"Me Ben," he announced, and launched himself into his father's arms.

* * *

Kerry threw several small items of clothing into a bag and returned to the kitchen in less than five minutes, hoping Ben hadn't managed to deposit too many chocolaty fingerprints on Pierce's pale sweater and slacks in the meantime. Her heart was thudding like a sledgehammer when she pushed open the door. She was terrified she had already left Pierce alone with George for too long. Terrified he would have already learned the answer to the question she had seen in his eyes as he carried Ben into the kitchen.

To her amazement all was quiet as Ben examined the intricacies of Pierce's watch. Even Lauren, safe in the familiar protection of George's arms, was wide-eyed with interest as Pierce pressed a high-pitched alarm.

Kerry's heart contracted. This was what it should have been like; Pierce, the children and herself; a real family. She stood silently in the doorway watching them, surprised by Pierce's patience as he obligingly pressed the alarm again, and then again, to squeals of excited laughter. He was smiling and his voice was softer than usual as he talked to the children, directing his remarks mainly to Ben but occasionally including Lauren so she was gradually losing her initial fright. For once silent, George watched approvingly as if he knew his own jocular behavior would be overshadowed by this interesting stranger who didn't seem at all put out by the smears of chocolate on his otherwise pristine clothes.

When George looked up and saw her standing in the doorway, he grinned. "Loyalty counts for nothing in the face of modern technology," he said. "I can't compete with a…what did you say it was Pierce?"

"An android smart watch. It works like a mini computer."

She tried to smile as she recalled how Pierce had always had to have the latest piece of equipment but when she looked at him the expression on his face ripped her apart. His eyes, which had been soft and blue as he talked to the children, hardened into slivers of grey as he stood up, balancing Ben easily on one arm.

"We'll finish our discussion tomorrow." His curt tone probably sounded businesslike to George but Kerry heard the threat in it and her hands started shaking again as she took Ben from him. He was telling her he knew Ben and Lauren were his and that their next discussion would be long and very painful. He was also telling her she had better have some good answers ready for the questions she could see in his eyes.

Her response was too bright as she moved towards the door. "Tomorrow will be fine but you'll have to excuse us right now because there's a meal waiting for us."

George stood up with a smile. "And knowing my wife there's bound to be a treat involved too which might spoil if we're late."

He held out his hand to Pierce. "It's been a pleasure to meet you. I wish I knew why you seem so familiar though. It'll keep me awake tonight trying to figure it out. Are you sure we haven't met before?"

"Positive. I just look like someone you know," Pierce didn't go into the Pierce Simon, famous tennis player routine that Kerry had seen so often in the past. Instead he picked up her bag and followed them through to the front door. The periwinkle blue eyes he shared with the twins, right down to the thick rim of lashes and straight black brows, were on Kerry as he spoke.

* * *

"What a pleasant young man," George glanced across at Kerry as he turned on the ignition and started the car. "He said you are friends from way back and that you met up again today by chance."

She nodded wearily. She supposed she should feel glad Pierce hadn't elaborated. Instead she just felt numb. She could still see the tail lights of his car as he accelerated away from them, and as she watched them dwindle into the distance she remembered his parting shot with an inward shiver. He'd waited until she had strapped Ben and Lauren into the car seats George had fitted into his car and closed the door. Then he had seized her arm. She'd flinched as his fingers bit into the soft flesh.

"Be here at eight o'clock tomorrow evening."

Nothing else. Not a smile or even a scowl. Just that implacable stare, the one she'd seen him give opponent after opponent as he faced them across the net. The one that meant he intended to win come what may. And now it was her turn to face him. He wanted his questions answered and he wasn't going to be satisfied until they were, and although she was terrified by the thought of what he might say and do, she knew she had no choice. She owed him an explanation.

"He certainly has a way with children," George interrupted her dark thoughts by nodding towards the back seats where the twins were sitting quietly, their thumbs plugged into their mouths as the days activities finally caught up with them. "Unusual in a fellow like that, his interest in children. He looks more the playboy type, all wild hair and jewelry if you know what I mean."

"Oh I do. I know exactly what you mean," Kerry gave a bitter laugh as he pulled up in Mel's driveway so she could collect the van. "And you're not wrong George. He is the playboy type except when it suits him to pretend to be something else."

"Past romance hmm?" He gave her a knowing look and then patted her hand as she nodded reluctantly. "Don't worry. I won't tell Mary or she'll have you married off in no time. She's always on about the twins needing a father."

"Since when do I have the time to go looking?" She managed a lop-sided grin. As he returned her smile George's air of puzzlement subsided. She was just tired, not upset. As usual he'd been imagining things. He'd put two and two together and made five when he'd first seen her with that young man but there was obviously nothing in it. Dismissing Pierce from his mind he asked her the question he'd been mulling over in his mind for the past hour or so.

"Would it help if the children stayed with us for the next couple of days while you stand in for Mel? You look all in as it is, so trying to cope with her work as well as your own is downright ridiculous. You need some help. Let Mary and me take Ben and Lauren off your hands for a day or two and give ourselves some pleasure into the bargain."

She shook her head doubtfully. "I don't know. They haven't ever been away from me overnight before, and besides, you already do far too much for me."

"Nonsense! You know how much we enjoy spending time with them. And we'd bring them home straight away if they started to miss you." He'd been searching through his pockets as he spoke and he finally located the spare set of van keys he always carried. He handed them over to her.

"Helping out with Ben and Lauren makes us feel useful you know. And they're such a delight at this age. You make the most of those two for as long as you can my dear. Take it from me, children grow up far too quickly."

His words pricked Kerry's conscience as she climbed into the van and started it up. He was right. She knew Ben and Lauren were fast leaving babyhood behind and she already regretted she wasn't able to devote more time to them, but her love for her children was at constant war with her need for money. With a heavy sigh she eased out of Mel's driveway and followed George's car down the road. There was really no solution to her predicament except to keep on working and to let George and Mary supply additional stability and love as proxy grandparents.

Fleetingly she recalled Pierce's parents. She'd only met them once, at Wimbledon, but she had immediately been aware of the strong bond of affection between them and Pierce; a warmth that had included her because she was with him. She felt an uncomfortable twinge of shame as, for the first time, she thought about his plump gray-haired mother and tall, taciturn father, and realized how much they would have loved to spend time with Ben and Lauren.

Abruptly she blinked back the tears that suddenly welled up into her eyes and forced herself to concentrate on the road. It was ridiculous to pine for what might have been when there had never been any question of building a future with Pierce. He had never hidden the fact that his career came first. Never pretended the future held anything more than constant travel as he pursued his dreams. He'd laughed at those players who had wives and children, telling Kerry it was madness, that the tennis circuit was the wrong place for families. She had agreed with him, the same as she had agreed they were both far too young to settle down. Then she had found out she was pregnant and had to grow up fast.

Her decision to leave him before he could accuse her of trapping him or being a burden or, worst of all, offering to pay for an abortion, had been made while she was still coming to terms with her pregnancy. Later she had sometimes wished she'd behaved differently but by then it was too late, and by then she had also learned that regret was a useless and destructive emotion. She needed to remember it now and put what had happened in the past behind her. She had to fight for what her life had become.

She also knew it would be far better for the twins if they spent a few days with George and

Mary while she attempted to explain her actions to Pierce.

* * *

The evening was uneventful. Mary and Kerry bathed the children and then George took charge of the bedtime story in Mel's old bedroom. It took slightly longer than usual to settle them but that was only because they were excited by the novelty of sleeping in a new bed. As far as Kerry could tell, they weren't worried about her leaving them at all. She smiled as she kissed them goodnight.

"Be good for Mary and George won't you?"

"Me good girl," Lauren said, and then she turned around and wriggled right down to the bottom of the bed so that Kerry couldn't see her.

"An' me!" Ben followed her until only his feet were visible.

Kerry laughed as she tickled his toes. "Is that why you're upside down? Is that where all the good children live?"

Smothered giggles issued from the tangle of bedclothes as Kerry's fingers found a sensitive spot on Ben's foot. Searching among the wriggling lumps and bumps under the covers she started to tickle Lauren too. Finally, with their faces red from their exertions and their hair ruffled, the children resurfaced and flung themselves at her. After several more kisses Kerry settled them onto their pillows and tucked them in. Then she tidied the toys they had scattered around the room and picked up their dirty clothes. By the time she had finished they were asleep.

She stood beside Mel's old double bed and watched them, seeing Pierce in the curving sweep of their eyelashes, their dark eyebrows, and the exuberant crest of their curls. Then her jaw tightened. They might look a lot like him but that didn't give him any rights over them. They were hers. They'd been hers from the moment she had learned that Pierce really didn't want children.

It had been immediately after she'd taken a third pregnancy test, hoping against hope it would show negative. Finally, reconciled to the inevitable, she had gone searching for Pierce, hoping that when he knew she was pregnant he would feel differently about the future. When she eventually found him he was leaning against a bar, beer glass in hand, laughing and joking with a group of tennis players. His doubles partner saw her first.

David Masters had known Kerry for almost as long as Pierce had, and he grinned at her as she walked towards them. "A good job you haven't reached the broody stage yet Kerry because Pierce is on his high horse again. He thinks dragging children around the tennis circuit is akin to child abuse!"

"I did not say that," when Pierce realized Kerry was standing behind him he turned around and dropped his arm across her shoulders. "I don't even think that. I just said it's not for me. I'm too selfish. If I became a father right now I would resent the baby every time it woke me up at night, every time it prevented me from doing something I wanted to do, every time I lost a match because I was tired. I don't have any problem with players who make different choices, I just know what's right for me."

Then he'd pulled Kerry close and kissed the top of her head. "Fortunately Kerry feels the same way don't you sweetheart, so for the foreseeable future we're both going to keep enjoying ourselves without a care in the world."

A shudder went right through Kerry as she recalled his words. How she had survived the rest of the evening she didn't know. After three years it was a blur. She guessed she must have smiled and nodded though. She might even have agreed with him while all the time she had been making plans to leave him, making plans to keep the baby growing inside her whether he wanted it or not. It was only later she found out it wasn't just one baby, but two, but by then her whole world had fallen apart anyway.

She leaned down and brushed some curls away from Lauren's flushed face. Then her fingers trailed across to where Ben was lying so she could touch him too. She wasn't going to let Pierce spoil all this, not now she had put her heart back together piece by fragile piece. Ben and Lauren were healthy, happy and well cared for. She was happy too, or she would be if she wasn't always so tired. She was proud of herself as well. She had done all this without any help from anyone, so commitment phobic Pierce Simon could go hang and she would tell him exactly that when she next saw him.

* * *

Later, over dinner, the conversation was desultory because everyone was tired and George and Mary didn't try to detain Kerry when she said it was time for her to leave. Mary merely kissed her and reminded her to leave some of the twin's clothes in her front porch for George to collect the following day.

"Not much," she called as she waved Kerry goodbye. "Just some extra sweaters and their boots. I can wash everything else through each evening."

* * *

Kerry drove home slowly, wondering how she was going to cope with the next few days and wishing Mel had chosen any other time to be ill. Meeting Pierce so unexpectedly after years of constant tiredness had pushed her to a breaking point and although she was determined to fight him tooth and nail, she wasn't sure how well she would be able to hold up against his angry questions. Her only hope was that a good night's sleep would give her the chance to build up some emotional resistance but it was something she was destined never to find out because when she arrived home, he was waiting for her.

She saw his car as soon as she turned the van into her road and she pushed her foot down hard on the accelerator in panic. He didn't give her the chance to even consider driving past, however. Instead he stepped out of his own car and stood in the middle of the otherwise deserted road, waiting for her to park. Then he walked up to the driver's door and yanked it open.

"You said tomorrow," she played for time, her thoughts befuddled by tiredness.

"I changed my mind," he reached in and half lifted, half pulled her from the driving seat. "You've already disappeared from my life once without any warning so I decided against giving you a second opportunity, especially as it would also involve my children."

He held her against the van with one hand and wrenched her chin up with the other, forcing her to look at him. "Don't even think about trying to deny it. I know they are my children and I guess they are also the reason your father threw you out. I would even hazard a guess they're the reason you disappeared from my life. What I don't understand is why. My god Kerry! How could you do it? Didn't you think I had any rights in the matter?"

She nodded miserably feeling hysterical sobs building up in her chest as his fingers bit into her upper arms. She would have given anything to be able to deny his claim on Ben and Lauren but to do that she would have to run faster and further. Maybe even change country. She started to tremble as reaction set in.

Pierce, however, was too furious to notice anything. His eyes glittered angrily under the streetlights and when he raised one arm she flinched because she thought he was going to hit her.

He released her instantly, the color draining from his face and leaving him white and drawn. His voice was heavy with bitterness as he stared down at her. "So that's what you think of me! Is that what all those months together taught you…that I am a total bastard?"

She shook her head, whispering her reply from a throat tight with tears. "I just thought you were mad about Ben and Lauren. I wouldn't…wouldn't have b..b..blamed you."

"Well I would," his gaze was bleak. "I don't hit women Kerry, so you can unlock your front door and allow us to finish this discussion in private without any fear that I'll knock you about. But you are right about me being mad. I'm madder than I've ever been in my life, and that's saying some, so if you know what's good for you you'll listen to what I'm going to say without interruption."

Slowly she turned towards the house, knowing when she was beaten, but he caught at her arm and pulled her back. There was a new menace in his voice as he peered through the windows of the van. "Haven't you forgotten something?"

For the first time she felt a faint surge of triumph, the shadowy return of some of her old spirit. "If you mean the children, then no. They're staying with George and Mary for a few days."

"Because you don't want them to see me or because you're too busy to look after them yourself?" His anger was ready to erupt again but this time she didn't flinch.

"Both. You already know I have to cover for my partner for a couple of days until she recovers from her sickness bug. If I try to look after Ben and Lauren at the same time then they'll suffer, so I've agreed they should stay with George and Mary. Also I'm not about to let my children get caught up in any arguments between us," she challenged him with her possessiveness.

"Is that so?" The bleakness in his eyes was replaced by a cold calculation, "Well I'm not prepared to have my children farmed out to just anyone because their mother doesn't have time to look after them."

"It has nothing whatsoever to do with you. Besides George and Mary aren't just anyone. They've known Ben and Lauren since they were babies. They're like grandparents to them."

"If that's supposed to make me feel better then you need to think again, because I'm not disposed to feel kindly towards people who have spent two years enjoying what was mine

65

by right, to say nothing of the fact that I could have supplied them with real grandparents." He tightened his grip on her arm as he steered her down the front path to the darkened recess of the porch.

"If you cared about them at all then you'd be pleased they're being well looked after," Kerry went on the defensive so she didn't have to listen to the truth behind his accusation.

"I've only your word for that, and frankly I have very little faith in your word, or even in your suitability to bring up my children." Pierce took her keys and opened the front door. He clicked the light switch in her hallway, flooding them both with the orange glow that shone through the cheap plastic shade.

* * *

Kerry stared up at him in disbelief. He couldn't mean it. It was anger talking. How could he possibly doubt her? He'd seen the twins, seen how happy and healthy they were. Surely she was just imagining the threat behind his words.

He returned her startled gaze implacably. "You don't have any choice Kerry. Either you marry me so they have two parents, or I'll fight you through the courts for them."

She felt her legs begin to give way beneath her as she stumbled through to the sitting room. His words whirled round and round in her head. Marry him! The thought was total madness. The shock of discovering he was a father must have temporarily deranged him.

She sank down onto the lumpy couch and put her head in her hands. She felt sick. Pierce sat down beside her and watched the changing expressions on her face as fear and disbelief mingled with incredulity and horror. When he was sure she was capable of listening he spoke again, but this time slowly and calmly as if he was dealing with a particularly recalcitrant child.

"I meant what I said Kerry. I won't have my children living like this when I can offer them so much more. Nor will I expose them to the sort of media gossip that will ensue if the story of their first two years gets out. They are my children and they will bear my name, as will their mother. We will be married by special license at the end of the week."

She raised her head and stared at him. "You can't make me."

"True. But I can drag you through the courts if you refuse…and believe me I will."

"So my wishes don't come into it?" She felt herself rallying as a rising anger gave her the strength to fight back.

"Why should they? You didn't take my wishes into account when Ben and Lauren were born."

"That was different and you know it," she flared back at him, pulling herself as far away from him as she could on the sagging couch. "Children were the last thing you wanted on the tennis circuit. You were always going on about it. They came slightly below a wife if I remember correctly, and that was pretty well at the bottom of the list. If I'd stayed with you and had the children it wouldn't have been long before they…we…started to cramp your style. Being a father would have ruined the image of the great Pierce Simon love machine."

Their eyes caught and held, anger fizzing between them in great bursts of tension while Pierce assimilated the ferocity of her challenge. Then his eyes darkened. "We can discuss the past later. This is about what happens now. You can forget your childish accusations as well because the tennis circuit is two years behind me. I'm living in an apartment at Greenleas at the moment while I wait for my house to be completed. I also have a stable lifestyle and enough money to ensure Ben and Lauren are properly cared for if you want to cavort about town playing at a career instead of looking after them."

"That's not fair! You can see I have to work to keep a roof over their heads."

"No I can't. As far as I'm concerned you have never needed to work. There was always enough money to care for all three of you. It was entirely your decision to turn your back on it at a considerable cost to our children, and without giving me any choice along the way."

He stood up and looked around the room as he finished speaking, his gaze taking in the shabby furniture, obviously second or even third

68

hand, the threadbare carpet and the cheap curtains. Kerry knew it was all scrupulously clean. Her worn fingers bore plenty of evidence of late night housekeeping but despite that, and her attempts to brighten it up with cheerful cushions, it still looked poor; poor and bare, with few ornaments and only one picture, a snapshot of the twins at a few months old.

Pierce saw it and with a muttered exclamation he walked across to the mantelpiece and picked it up. The corners were curled and there was a fingerprint smudge where Ben had once seized it with sticky hands. He studied it for a long time and when he finally turned around he was still holding it, his eyes unreadable.

"Take it or leave it Kerry. Either marry me or fight me for the children in court."

* * *

Kerry groaned as her alarm clock dragged her out of a fitful sleep. She had tossed and turned for most of the night, too inhibited by the fact that Pierce had taken over her couch to even get up to make a hot drink. Exhaustion had finally won out as the familiar street noises began outside the window and now, less than two hours later, it was time to get up. She put out an anxious hand and stopped the alarm before it could disturb Pierce. Then she pushed back the duvet and sat on the edge of the bed.

In blue cotton pajamas and with rumpled hair and her cheeks still flushed with sleep she looked like a child herself; far too young to be responsible for two-year-old twins; but inside she felt a hundred years old as she reflected on her future. Although Pierce had said little more the previous evening she knew he meant what he said. If she wanted to keep the twins and avoid the sort of heartbreak a court case might bring, then she had to marry him.

He had made it very plain that any reluctance on her part would drive him to instant legal action, and she knew she couldn't compete. With his money and contacts he would win hands down. After all what court would give exclusive custody to an single mother who had quite deliberately hidden her children's existence from their father, subjecting them to a life of near poverty when she knew he was capable of providing for their every need? Her reasons for leaving him would be dismissed as childish whims, and the fact that her own father had disowned her would also be seen as further evidence of her unsuitability to care for the children on her own. Worse, even though Pierce had left the tennis world behind him, his public profile would still win him the sympathy of all his fans while she would be publicly castigated as the woman who had deprived him of his right to be a father.

She had no choice. She had to marry him if she wanted Ben and Lauren. She rested her head in her hands as she contemplated the bleakness of such a loveless union. What did he expect to gain from marrying her? Why not just fight for the children anyway? She gave a dry sob.

"Kerry," Pierce pushed open the bedroom door and walked across to where she was sitting. He was carrying a mug of coffee. He was barefoot and his chin was dark with stubble. He looked awful, as if he, too, had been lying awake all night contemplating a miserable future.

"What do you want?" She made a grab for her robe and pulled it around her shoulders as she stared at his bare chest and the golden hair that tapered to a V where his waist narrowed into unbelted slacks.

"I heard your alarm and thought this might help," he held out the mug with an expression that had lost some of the previous night's animosity. "Come on, drink it up, it'll make you feel better."

"Nothing will make me feel better except to be left in peace in my own home," she ignored the mug as she concentrated on buttoning her robe right up to the neck.

"We've already discussed that, so you may as well reconcile yourself to the fact that I'm not letting you out of my sight until we're married," he was patient rather than irritated as he placed the mug of coffee on the corner of the bedside table.

"Not even if I promise to bring the children to see you every day?" She tried bribery without much hope of success.

"Not even then. Your track record on staying around isn't good enough." His wry smile acknowledged her ploy as he left the room.

She summoned up her few remaining dregs of courage and pulled a face at his retreating back. Then she reached for the coffee and drank it reluctantly, trying not to feel grateful as it eased her parched throat.

Chapter Four

It didn't take Kerry long to shower and pull on a pair of faded denims and a warm sweater, but by the time she padded downstairs the breakfast was ready.

"I'm not entirely clueless so you can stop looking so dumbfounded," Pierce said when he saw her surprise. He was fully dressed now and apart from needing a shave looked far too presentable, the weariness she had noticed earlier banished by cold water and strong coffee. A familiar surge of annoyance washed over her as she sat opposite him at the table. He had always been the same, had always been able to look fresh and ready for anything however hard he'd been living the night before. And from the glimpse of neatly folded blankets through the half open doorway, she saw he had even found the time to tidy up the couch as well.

He placed a plate of scrambled eggs in front of her with an attempt at humor. "You can forget the tennis circuit king now. This is the real Pierce Simon, egg-scrambler deluxe!"

She eyed her breakfast distastefully, refusing to respond with the smile he was looking for. "Aren't I to be allowed any choices at all now? You know I don't eat a cooked breakfast, or maybe you've forgotten that too just like you seem to have forgotten all the things you said in the past."

"I told you we're not going there, Kerry," he warned as he poured her a fresh mug of coffee. "Besides that was when you weren't all skin and bone with dark circles under your eyes. You don't look as if you've fed yourself properly for months and as your future husband I intend to do something about it."

"I thought Ben and Lauren were your only concern," she pushed the egg moodily around her plate until he put out his hand and stopped her.

"You are their mother. I owe it to them to make sure you're fit enough to look after them," his voice was unexpectedly gentle as he trapped her cold fingers beneath his own, stopping her restless movements.

"Last night you wrote me off as a hopeless case, not to be trusted with them," she raised her eyes to his, her expression mutinous until he started chafing her hands between his own to rub some warmth into them. Instantly her pulse slowed and she felt the traitorous leap of her heart. Hastily she snatched them away before all her old feelings returned and overwhelmed her.

He sighed as he picked up his knife and fork. "Yesterday I was too angry to think straight but thanks to your very inhospitable couch, I've spent most of the night awake going over everything you told me. I know you've done a fine job. Ben and Lauren are lovely children and I'm going to be proud of them but that doesn't mean I can ignore the fact you appear to be systematically wearing your fingers down to the bone. There's no need for that now Kerry. I can look after all three of you and give you all the time you need to rest and regain your bloom."

She gave a bitter laugh. "For what? For a marriage that's being forced on me! Is that my part of the bargain Pierce? Do I have to work hard at becoming an attractive accessory again?"

His expression hardened. "I might have known better than to expect you to meet me half way. All right, let's set out our terms while you're in such a picky frame of mind but while we're doing so, don't forget this marriage has been forced on both of us. I would never have chosen to start married life with a ready made family."

She pushed away her half eaten breakfast and stared at him. "What do you mean, terms?"

He shrugged. "Well we can't rely on good old-fashioned love can we, so the sooner we agree on a set of rules the better. We need to agree how best to keep Ben and Lauren safe and happy while we work through our own problems."

She clenched her fists. How could he think like that? Didn't he know that people rarely followed rules when emotions were involved? Of course he did! It was what he was saying. He was telling her that because his emotions weren't involved it was going to be easy to agree to some sort of routine. A plan that would leave them both free to live their own lives whilst ensuring Ben and Lauren had a stable home.

She felt the brittle object inside her that she supposed was her mended heart begin to break in two again as she realized her three years of struggle had gained her nothing. She would soon be trapped inside the sort of marriage she'd been running from when she walked out on Pierce. She could still remember the painful soul searching she'd gone through before she cut him out of her life; how she'd tried to balance his right to know about her pregnancy with his distaste for anything domestic, especially children. In the end she'd decided to tell him and had gone looking for him, hoping against hope that once he knew she was pregnant his attitude would change. She would have told him too if she hadn't walked into that jokey discussion in the bar, the one that had broken her heart at the same time it made up her mind for her.

One thing her mother had taught her before she died was that whatever happened in life you always had to accept the consequences of your actions. And because it was her own forgetfulness that made her pregnant, Kerry had decided the responsibility for her babies was hers alone. She had also decided she wasn't going to subject her children to the same sort of childhood she had known. As far as she was concerned a life without a father would be infinitely preferable to living with one who didn't want them. She wouldn't subject them to the same sort of misery she had suffered.

There had been something else too and even in the worst moments after she'd left him, even when her father had delivered the final blow that almost broke her, it hadn't changed. She had never begrudged Pierce his freedom.

Hiding Ben and Lauren's existence from him had been her final act of love because she didn't want to do what her mother had done. She didn't want to turn him into a reluctant father with no time or patience for his children...except that suddenly it wasn't like that anymore. Now her world was falling about her ears because this new Pierce Simon did seem to have time for his children after all, and quite a lot of patience too.

She closed her eyes as she tried to come to terms with the change in him and wondered again why he'd turned his back on his career. Maybe if she'd followed his matches after she left him she'd understand, but it was the one thing she hadn't been able to do. One brief glimpse of him on a sporting highlights program had convinced her of that, and she had never watched tennis again.

"It's not that difficult. All we need are a few ground rules Kerry, not a full length thesis," his biting remark brought her back to the breakfast table with a start.

She opened her eyes and gave him an apologetic shrug. "My mind was drifting. Sorry."

His voice softened slightly. "No suggestions then?"

She shook her head.

"No rules about housekeeping, or tidiness. No stipulations about the children's bedtime and how many sweets they're allowed to eat?" He was teasing now and there was a shadow of the old Pierce in the blue gleam of his eyes but she felt too tired to respond, and it wasn't because of her broken night. It was because of the deep down, grinding weariness that was the result of three years of managing alone. After a moment he seemed to sense it because he stood up and started to clear the table.

"Not to worry. We can discuss it later at Greenleas."

His mention of the sports complex brought her to her senses with a gasp of horror. "What time is it? I'm meant to be laying out a buffet in the church hall down by the shore by eleven o'clock."

He frowned. "Find someone else to do it. We've a wedding to arrange."

"You've a wedding to arrange," she corrected icily. "And just to make things easier for you, I don't give a damn about the arrangements so you can do what you like. I do care about Mel though and I won't let her down. You heard me talking to her on the phone last night so you know I promised to help out."

"That was before you had problems of your own."

"Well at least you admit to being a problem," Kerry was surprised to find a smile creeping across her face because suddenly Pierce looked exactly like Ben when he couldn't have his own way.

He glared at her. "What's so funny?"

"You are. You look just like Ben when he's having a tantrum. I always wondered where he learned that ferocious scowl," she couldn't stop grinning.

Her unexpected amusement broke the tension between them. Pierce returned her smile with a wry grin.

"It can't be taught. It's genetic."

"So is obstinacy," she reverted to their quarrel with a shake of her head. "And I intend to go to work whether you like it or not. Besides, there isn't anyone else."

Surprisingly he gave in. "Okay but there's plenty of time yet so you can relax because with two of us it won't take so long."

"You don't mean…you're not expecting to come with me?" She stared at him in amazement as she pictured the incongruity of Pierce Simon helping out at a conference buffet.

He gave a sudden grin. "Why not? It's a long time since I went to the seaside."

"Oh do be sensible! You'll be bored out of you mind while I'm working. For goodness sake go back to Greenleas and leave me alone Pierce.

I won't run away…I haven't the strength these days."

"You know I'm almost inclined to believe you, so let's just say I'm coming with you because I think you need some help," he finished stacking the plates in the sink and then returned to the table and pulled her to her feet. He stilled her protest by placing a finger on her lips.

"No! No arguments. We go together or you don't go at all."

Kerry gave in after one look at the determined expression on his face. She knew when she was beaten. There would be no further concessions.

* * *

"It says turn right at the next set of traffic lights," Kerry glanced at the instructions she was holding and then looked at the road ahead. The traffic lights were about three hundred yards ahead of them. Pierce flicked the van's indicator switch and then slowly pulled across to the outside lane of the dual carriageway.

Within minutes they had turned into the car park of a barn-like building bearing the legend St Michael's Hall in faded green letters. Pierce killed the engine and then frowned at Kerry.

"Were you going to tackle all those steps on your own or are you expecting some help from the people who own the hall?"

She shook her head. "I don't know. This is Mel's thing, not mine. I should have checked with her. I usually just supply the food."

"I guess Mel must be a seven foot Amazon then," he suggested hopefully, his mood so unexpectedly light-hearted that Kerry found herself smiling at such an unlikely picture.

"She's bigger than me."

He grinned at her. "Now that is not exactly a miracle of biology. You may be many things Kerry, but big is not one of them!"

She pulled a face. "Surely you know the best things come in small packages!"

"Did I ever say differently?" Suddenly tension was back, easing between them, flowing from his fingers as he put his hand on her arm. It was a different tension though. A tension brought back by a familiar repartee about her fragile five foot three frame. It was something he'd often teased her about and her indignant retaliations had nearly always ended in lovemaking, with Pierce very effectively proving to her exactly how he thought small was beautiful. A whole history of memories was between them now, binding them together in the close confines of the van.

She deliberately smashed them with a brittle laugh. "Come on, we've a lot to do before twelve o'clock."

* * *

They finished at three-thirty. Pierce loaded the last empty box onto the van with a sigh of relief.

"That's one way I really wouldn't like to earn my living. Are you serious about this Kerry, or is it just a way of earning a crust?" He shut the rear doors with a weary shake of his head.

"A crust just about sums it up," she gave a tired little shrug as she waited for him to unlock the passenger door. "But it is important to me because it's something Mel and I have achieved on our own."

He frowned. "What if I said I didn't approve and I wanted you to give it all up?"

"I couldn't," her answer was prompt. "Mel relies on me, and I owe her. Besides, I enjoy cooking. It's the only thing I'm really good at."

"Then you'd better talk to Mel about running the whole thing out of Greenleas. It'll be simpler if you're both working in the same building, and I'm sure I can find you an office as well as some kitchen space. You can even have a go at running the snack bar in the Spa if you like. You might prefer it to what you're doing at the moment and there's a lot of potential for expansion. The members are always saying they'd like to be able to buy more than coffee and donuts without having to use the main restaurant. Mind you, if you do decide to take it over it will have to run like clockwork."

"You're not offering us any favors then?"

"Damn right I'm not! I run a business not a charity and the minute you're not up to scratch, you're out."

Kerry gave him a sharp look, not quite daring to believe what he'd just offered her. "In that case aren't you being a bit premature? You haven't even met Mel yet, and yesterday I showed you the sort of mess I can get myself into. You're taking an awful lot on trust Pierce, especially for somewhere as upmarket as Greenleas."

To her surprise he grinned at her as he climbed into the driver's seat. "Don't forget I'll be living with one of the partners. That has to be some sort of security. Are you interested or not?"

She nodded hesitantly. "I think so. I'll have to talk it over with Mel of course, but it's exactly the sort of opportunity we've been looking for. What sort of food are you thinking of?"

He fitted the key into the ignition. "It's up to you. Once the centre opens officially it won't just be gym and spa members either. You'll be overrun with customers from the hotel as well as the conference centre. And later there will be a golf course, and kids from the tennis school."

"And you really think we can handle it?" She stared at him wide-eyed as he pulled out of the car park.

"The food we served today was very good, so I'm prepared to give you a chance. And you don't have to do it all on your own. Call in other experts; take on some more staff if you have to. Anything as long as it works."

They travelled several miles in silence while Kerry digested his offer. It was the chance she and Mel had been looking for and although, despite his denial, it smacked of charity, she knew it suited him sufficiently for her to have few qualms about accepting. If she was going to marry him then she was going to accept his dowry as well.

She wondered what Mel's reaction would be, both to Pierce and to his offer, and decided her friend would be in favor of both. Pierce because he would provide the children with a much needed father, and Greenleas because it was another step up the ladder of her ambition.

She smiled. Mel was an enigma. Tallish and blondish, she was physically very ordinary, and yet she still somehow managed to look a million dollars whatever the situation, while her languid manner hid an abundance of energy that Kerry had only ever seen surpassed by Pierce. And like Pierce, her energy was never wasted. It was always directed towards whatever project she was working on, which right now was to run a very successful catering company. Well, it seemed as if her long awaited chance was coming. No more hit and miss affairs as they struggled to service small local conferences. Instead they would be managing their very own bistro with all mod cons thrown in.

"Let's stop at Mel's on the way home?"

"Why do I have the feeling this has nothing to do with our forthcoming wedding and everything to do with Greenleas?" Pierce gave a wry smile as he obediently followed her directions, and before long they had parked in her friend's driveway and climbed down from the van.

Mel opened the door before Kerry had time to ring the bell. She stared at Pierce.

Kerry blushed as she introduced him, only now realizing how difficult her explanation was going to be. "This is Pierce."

"I know who he is," Mel shook her head in disbelief. "Why didn't you tell Dad you were Pierce Simon when you met him? He's been muttering all day about how he's sure he's met you before."

All this was delivered in Mel's usual forthright manner as she proffered an elegantly manicured hand. Pierce took it with a grin, clicked his heels together and bowed low.

She chuckled. "I'm immune to that sort of behavior. Save it for Kerry. She's much more gullible."

"I know she is. That's why she's going to marry me next Saturday," Pierce dropped the bombshell without preamble and then, before she could respond, he elaborated. "And we've come to tell you I'm bringing a dowry."

* * *

At first Mel thought he was joking but a second look at Kerry made her think again. She stared at both of them with a bewildered expression on her face.

"You don't mean this coming Saturday!"

Kerry nodded her head miserably. She'd been so full of the opportunity Pierce was offering them, so glad she could begin to repay Mel for her friendship, that she'd pushed the thought of her forthcoming wedding to the back of her mind. Now, faced with Mel's bewilderment, the sheer impossibility of it all washed over her again and left her speechless. Pierce stepped into the silence.

"We knew one another years ago. We're just picking up where we left off."

"But this Saturday…it's all so sudden. Why the hurry? And what about Ben and Lauren? Surely they need more time to adjust."

"I…they like Pierce," Kerry felt tears choke in her throat. How was she going to explain to Mel she'd been living a lie? How was she going to tell her and Mary and George she was a single mother by choice, not because the father of her children had abandoned her? It made her feel cheap and mean in the face of their generous support. She searched desperately for the right words, her eyes pleading instinctively with Pierce. He gave a slight smile.

"Children are very adaptable and I'll let them get used to me gradually."

"Ben can be a handful!"

His smile widened. "An obstacle I'll deal with when I come to it. Now are you ready to hear about my offer or are you going to keep us on the doorstep for the rest of the afternoon?"

* * *

They drove to Greenleas in silence, Kerry because she was emotionally exhausted and Pierce because he seemed to be lost in a world of his own. Neither of them spoke until he'd parked Mel's van next to his Mercedes at the far end of the car park.

"Why didn't you tell Mel you are the children's father?" Kerry twisted her hands together in her lap, her voice little more than a whisper as she ventured the question that had been haunting her for the past two hours.

Pierce paused in the act of opening the driver's door and glanced across at her. "Because she's your friend so I assumed you'd tell her if you wanted her to know."

Her expression was troubled. Why wasn't he angry when she'd not only taken away his fundamental right to parenthood but also denied it to him now?

"I didn't know how to tell her," she admitted, staring down at her tightly clasped fingers so she didn't have to look at him.

"It isn't important. As long as Ben and Lauren are under my legal protection I can wait for the rest." His hand was warm as it covered hers and she only gave a token resistance as he slipped an arm around her shoulders and pulled her to him.

His unexpected generosity, combined with the warmth of his body through his sweater, tipped Kerry over the brink and the tears she'd been holding back since the previous day welled up in her eyes. It had been a long time since anyone had held her like that. For too long she had had to be the strong one, coping with the children's baby illnesses and upsets alone, so suddenly the temptation to hand everything over to this new, caring Pierce, was very strong. He seemed to sense it because he held her even tighter as he tilted her face towards him.

"Let go Kerry. You're not on your own anymore."

It was dark now so she couldn't read the expression in his eyes. She could feel his lips though, as they brushed her forehead and then feathered their way down the soft curve of her cheek to claim her lips in a kiss that was neither demanding nor threatening. It was all that was needed to make the tears spill over. They trickled down her face and into their joined mouths. Immediately Pierce stopped kissing her and with an odd little groan pulled her head into the angle of his shoulder, making no attempt to talk to her until the worst of her tears were over. Then he opened the driver's door.

"Come on. Let's go and find something to eat. Everything always looks better from the outside of a hot meal."

Her attempted smile ended in a half sob as she climbed down from the passenger seat and followed him round to a side entrance that led straight into his private suite of rooms.

"Sit down and make yourself comfortable while I order some food. You look all in."

Obediently she did as he said, and then tried to hide the tears that were still trickling down her face by blowing her nose. He smiled at her.

"You'll soon feel better. Now what would you like to drink?"

She shook her head, not trusting herself to speak.

"Come on Kerry. It's not that bad. You'll get used to me again, I promise. And so will Ben and Lauren." He'd seen her fresh outburst of tears and he sat down beside her and pulled her round to face him.

But she couldn't answer him. Instead she scrubbed at her streaming eyes with a damp tissue and hoped that one day he would understand why she had behaved as she did, and forgive her. She also hoped she wouldn't get used to him too easily because if she did then she was going to have to face up to the fact she had never stopped loving him and wanting him, while all he wanted was Ben and Lauren.

Chapter Five

The next day passed in a whirl of organization as, ignoring Kerry's protests, Pierce took over Melanie's Kitchen, barking out instructions to his kitchen staff while they worked their way through Mel's list and menus.

By late morning, however, his patience finally gave way. "For goodness sake stop following me around Kerry. I know it's your company but with Mel sick and you too emotionally exhausted to cope, this is the only way it's going to work. Besides, it's keeping my kitchen staff occupied. Until the hotel and conference centre open up at the end of the month they've too much spare time on their hands. They are also perfectly capable of preparing and serving all the lunches you have booked for the rest of the week, so you don't need to worry."

"But there's nothing for me to do," Kerry continued to trail after him dejectedly as he strode around Greenleas issuing orders and checking on the almost completed building work. She wasn't used to having time on her hands and with the twins away and his staff taking over her workload, she felt unnecessary and unwanted. It was all very well for Pierce and Mel to agree it would be better if she rested until after the wedding; they didn't have her thoughts churning around inside their heads; thoughts she could only ignore if she was too busy to think.

Her obvious misery eventually got through to Pierce. With a long-suffering sigh he took her hand and marched her past the squash courts and the gym to the double wooden doors marked Spa. He thrust them open and ushered her through with a brief smile that barely hid his irritation.

"Maggie, I've a new customer for you," he addressed an attractive girl wearing a spotless white tabard and trousers. She was checking some figures at the reception desk but when the doors opened she looked up with a smile.

"Sauna, massage, manicure, pedicure, facial?"

"The works," he relaxed slightly and grinned. "Whatever it takes to unwind her. In fact don't let her out of here until you're sure she'll sleep for twenty-four hours straight."

"That bad hmm! Well you've picked a good time. As you can see, lunchtime on a Wednesday is not exactly our most busy period at the moment. You've the whole spa to yourself."

"But I don't want a sauna or a massage…or…or any of those other things," Kerry turned furiously to Pierce. She wished he would stop ordering her around like this when she was only tense and emotional because of him and his stupid ideas? What she actually needed was to talk to him, to try to find a way out of this ridiculous arrangement. The last thing she needed was a sauna or a massage. She began to tell him so but Pierce had already gone, leaving the doors swinging gently behind him.

"Well I knew he was anxious to improve business but I didn't realize he'd resorted to dragging unwilling customers in off the street! Come on, it isn't that bad," Maggie put her hands on her hips and grinned at Kerry.

Her smile was wide and friendly, inviting intimacy at Pierce's expense, and after a moment Kerry found herself responding with a resigned shrug. "Why not? I haven't anything else to do. Pierce has made sure of that."

"He must be suffering from withdrawal symptoms again," Maggie picked up a pile of fluffy white towels and indicated that Kerry should follow her.

"Withdrawal symptoms?" Kerry moved forward reluctantly.

The other girl laughed. "It happens quite regularly, usually when there's a crisis. We call it the 'I wish I was a tennis star again syndrome' and bow and scrape accordingly!"

When she saw Kerry's look of incomprehension she paused outside a door marked Treatment Room 1 and explained. "When he was the world's favorite tennis star everybody jumped to do his bidding. His coach kept problems to a minimum, especially just before a match, and he was cosseted and protected. He was allowed to be temperamental. It was even seen as a good thing if it fired him up to win. That all stopped when he retired though, and here at Greenleas the problems are all his. He's learned the hard way that being temperamental only makes them worse, so he copes by playing god whenever it gets too much for him. I don't know what you did, but you were obviously getting too much for him!"

"But that's not going to solve anything," Kerry was intrigued enough by this new insight into Pierce's behavior to stop thinking about her own problems for a brief moment.

"Oh it does. It prevents argument," Maggie held the door open with an inviting smile. "After all, you gave in about the spa didn't you?"

Kerry gave a wry smile as she accepted the cotton towel the other girl handed to her. "Does anybody ever stand up to him?"

"Not so you'd notice, except for Marissa Reynolds. When she's around and things don't go her way it's like the clash of the titans."

She didn't need to elaborate. Kerry's stomach turned a complete cartwheel when she heard Marissa's name. A willowy red head with endless legs and perfect American teeth, she had been a ranked player in the days when Kerry knew her. She had also been the darling of the media who couldn't get enough of her stunning figure, her wide green eyes, and the fact that the camera loved her. Despite never quite making the grade on the tennis circuit, she had rarely been out of the news as she posed beside the biggest stars, including Pierce, or modeled the new season's kit, or gave an interview about whatever was happening in her life. Kerry guessed nothing had changed except that she'd probably built a celebrity career for herself by now.

"Does she visit Greenleas often?" She concentrated on wrapping herself in the warm, scented towel while she waited for Maggie to answer.

"All the time when she's in England. In fact we're all taking bets she'll be Mrs Pierce Simon before long. If she doesn't wear him down it won't be for want of trying that's for sure...there's nothing subtle about Marissa."

Kerry stretched out on the massage table, loosened her towel and gave herself up to Maggie's ministrations as she thought about what she had just been told. If she was honest none of it was very surprising. It was inevitable Pierce would miss the applause and adulation of his fans just as much as he would miss the actual physical achievement of defeating opponent after opponent across the world. Nor should she be surprised Marissa Reynolds was back in his life because their names had been linked romantically long before Kerry met him.

She let her mind travel back to the heady days when she'd first met Pierce. Even then he'd had Marissa in tow. She remembered their first meeting. Pierce and Marissa had been attending a reception together as representatives of the competitors who were to take part in a tournament sponsored by her father's company. Kerry was there on sufferance. Although she was a keen amateur tennis player her father hadn't thought to include her and she'd had to beg for an invitation when she heard about the reception. Eventually, realizing her knowledge of tennis might be useful, he'd given in and she had dressed for the occasion with excited anticipation, taking more care than usual with her appearance because she was going to meet Pierce Simon.

He'd been everything the television screen had shown him to be, and more. Tall, slim, muscular, with flashing blue eyes and wild sun streaked hair, he had looked almost piratical. His teeth had gleamed in a sardonic smile as he bowed over her hand. He could pick out a fan at twenty paces.

She'd blushed, knowing he'd seen through her thin veneer of sophistication to the excited teenager beneath. Embarrassed at being found out, she'd concentrated on talking to his companion instead. Marissa, however, had little time for other women, especially young, pretty ones, so she had cold-shouldered Kerry in favor of her father. At fifty, he was almost twice Marissa's age but she didn't consider that a failing as he was still male and very attractive. Only Kerry knew his youthful looks and smooth skin were down to a discreet cosmetic surgeon.

She also knew it was something she must never, ever allude to.

Marissa made a fatal mistake by targeting Charles Farrow, however, because it left Pierce free to talk to Kerry. And Kerry, having discovered that some tennis stars had very mediocre manners, was in no mood to be trifled with. Her irritation amused him sufficiently to invite her to join them both for dinner later that evening. She had stared at him in disbelief.

"Hadn't you better check with Miss Reynolds first because somehow I don't think she'll be too thrilled by the idea?"

"It'll do Miss Reynolds good to know she's not the only fish in the sea," his answer had been a trifle grim even though he'd continued to smile. "Now are you going to accept my invitation Miss Kerry Farrow, or do I have to get down on bended knee?"

"I think I'd like the bended knee bit," she'd giggled and then clutched at his arm in mortification as he began to kneel. "No don't! Please don't! The Press photographers are here. They'll start taking photos."

He'd grinned at her. "Won't your publicity stand it?"

"My father won't stand it. It's his company that's sponsoring the tournament and I'm only here on sufferance. I'm meant to be on my best behavior."

"Your father?" He'd looked around with interest. "Is he the big guy with the silver hair? The one who's keeping Marissa sweet?"

She nodded, wondering if he minded the fact that Marissa was very definitely flirting with her father, but he'd only grinned.

"In that case, let's make it a family foursome. Let's go to the Boathouse," he'd name an extravagantly priced restaurant cum nightclub on the outskirts of town, and then wandered off to confirm the arrangements with the other two.

* * *

"I don't think I've ever treated someone as tense as you" Maggie's voice dragged Kerry's thoughts back from the past to the aromatic blend of massage oils and the long smooth strokes of Maggie's hands on her body.

"I...life is a bit difficult at the moment," Kerry admitted, obediently turning over so that the other girl could concentrate on her front.

"If I'd realized you were so uptight I'd have suggested a hot stone massage but it's a bit late for that now. How about having a sauna instead? Some of my clients like to loosen up their muscles by having one before I massage them. Afterwards can be just as effective though and it will have the added benefit of perking up your skin ready for the facial I'm going to give you later on. Aw come on! You may as well make the most of Pierce's generosity unless you've something better to do," she added when Kerry shook her head.

As Maggie continued to massage her back, Kerry felt herself go tense all over again at the other girl's words. That was exactly the problem. She didn't have anything else to do. Pierce had made sure of that. She couldn't even go and see Lauren and Ben without telling him because he still had the keys to the van and Greenleas was much too far away from a train station or even a bus stop to contemplate walking out on him. She could book a taxi of course, but if she did she would have to ask George to pay for it when she reached his house because it would cost far more than she had in her purse. She didn't rate her chances of getting away without Pierce seeing her go either. He'd probably put his receptionist on 'Kerry Watch' or something.

Maggie, sensing her indecision, made up her mind for her. "It'll be fine Kerry. You'll love it. And afterwards you can have a cool shower and then rest in the relaxation area while I make you a fruit cocktail to replace all the fluids you'll lose."

* * *

Kerry enjoyed the sauna more than she expected to. The dry heat seemed to seep right into her bones so that for the first time since Pierce had come back into her life she felt warm again. Stretching out on the towel she spread on the wooden slats, her mind drifted back to that magical evening again, to a time that now seemed more than a lifetime ago.

It had been obvious from the way Marissa ignored Pierce that she was furious with his plans. Sharing the spotlight with another woman was not how she had expected to spend her evening. Determined to punish him she flirted excessively with Charles Farrow. It was a ploy that turned out to be her final undoing though because it left the way clear for Pierce to take Kerry onto the dimly lit dance floor.

A visceral jolt of desire flooded her body as she remembered the first time he'd taken her in his arms. Dancing with him had been a revelation as his hands molded her to him, making her almost a part of him as he led her into the music. All awareness of her father and Marissa had drifted away, their cynical comments about the other diners no longer intrusive as Pierce became the centre of her existence. And by the time the music finally stopped she knew she'd had the same effect upon him. She knew he was equally reluctant to join the others and make polite conversation.

After that there had been no looking back. Flowers had arrived the following morning, flowers and a second invitation that did not include her father. The following two weeks had been a whirlwind of experiences – their first kiss; the day Pierce managed to escape the long lens of the photographers for long enough to take her to a hidden place and make love to her for the first time; the hours she'd spent wrapped in his arms while they watched his opponents lose; the thrill of knowing he was hers when he held up the winner's cup. By the time the tournament was over she had agreed to join him on the circuit as soon as she could. Then a photo of their very passionate farewell kiss made it to the front page of the national newspaper her father read every morning. When he saw it he was livid.

"That's the last time you attend one of my sponsorship events," he told her. "You've made Farrow Holdings a laughing stock Kerry, and I won't have it. From now on you'll concentrate on your job and keep out of the papers."

"But that's not fair! What's the difference between me seeing Pierce and you spending most of your time with Marissa?" she protested

"Marissa Reynolds has been fulfilling the requirements of the sponsorship deal by posing for photographs and attending cocktail parties while Pierce Simon has reneged on almost every part of the agreement. Instead he has put all his energy into trying to get into my daughter's knickers and succeeding too if that photo is anything to go by."

"It's not like that. He loves me, and he's asked me to join him on the circuit as soon as I can," she shouted, hating the way he made her relationship with Pierce seem sordid.

"You're far too young to understand love you silly girl. Pierce Simon is talking about lust, that's all it is…lust. He's making a fool of you

Kerry. How long do you think you can hold onto him? A week? A month?"

Resolutely ignoring the fact that Pierce had never actually told her he loved her, Kerry stood her ground. She was going with Pierce whether her father liked it or not. Life on the tennis circuit, even if it proved to be short lived, had to be better than sharing a house with a man who never bothered to disguise the fact that he found her presence irksome, and her ineptitude at the job she hated an affront to his own success.

Maggie popped her head through the door, interrupting her thoughts. "You've been in the sauna for nearly fifteen minutes Kerry. That's more than long enough for one session."

Her phone rang while she was speaking and with an apologetic smile she answered it. After a short conversation she cut the call, handed Kerry a soft cotton robe and made for the door.

"Sorry, but I've got to go. They're having a problem with some deliveries in reception. It's a whole lot of new stuff for the Spa but nobody can check it because the order form is missing. I won't be long. Just go through to the relaxation area when you're ready."

* * *

Dropping her towel and robe onto a nearby bench Kerry stood under the shower for several minutes, letting the lukewarm spray cool her skin. Then she saw the plunge pool and decided she may as well use that too. Maggie had told her the icy water would close all the pores in her skin and although she hadn't said to use it, it seemed a good idea to Kerry, especially if she was to have a facial later on. With a sharp intake of breath, she lowered herself into the water.

Although the shock of the cold water on her skin made her gasp, it didn't wash away her memories. If anything they were clearer than they had been for years and she guessed it was because she had nothing to do but to focus on them. Irritated with herself, and with Pierce for taking away everything that kept her too busy to think, she ducked her head beneath the water as she tried to forget the last words her father had thrown at her.

He had used language she had never heard from him before when she told him she was pregnant. Then, with his voice full of venom, he had told her to get out of his house. "If you won't have an abortion then I won't have you here flaunting his brat," he told her.

The memory ripped at her emotions even as she wondered why she had ever thought he would react differently. She'd been as naïve about him as she had been about Pierce and both of them had let her down.

* * *

"Kerry!" She could hear Pierce shouting at her but she decided to ignore him. He was a long way away, too far away for her to bother to listen to him while she was still trying to piece together the mysteries of her past. She ducked beneath the water again only to find herself hauled back to the surface by a grabbing hand. Spluttering indignantly she glared at Pierce. What was he doing in the pool fully dressed? Couldn't he see that his jeans were soaking wet?

"Leave me alone," she tried to kick him with her bare feet as he lifted her out of the pool and was surprised to find they didn't work. Nor did her fingers so she was forced to hang helplessly in his arms while he wrapped her in a thick towel and carried her back into the sauna.

"What were you trying to do you crazy little fool? Drown yourself? Surely getting married to me isn't that bad!" He dumped her unceremoniously onto the bench and kicked the door shut with his foot.

She started to shiver, her teeth chattering as she watched him strip off his jeans and polo shirt and rub himself briskly with a towel. He glanced across at her, his expression softening slightly as he reached for another towel.

"You'll be warmer in a minute. Here, let me rub your hands and feet," he draped the second towel around her shoulders and then knelt down and took one of her feet in his hands.

She watched in silence, feeling the warmth seep back into her body as the heat of the sauna began to build up in the cubicle. It beaded Pierce's shoulders with sweat so they gleamed gold under the dim light. He finished rubbing her feet and felt her hands.

"Better?"

"Yes thank you. I was just cooling down after the sauna. I didn't mean to stay in the pool," her throat felt tight as she tried to curl away from him.

He stood up and leaned against the door, apparently unaware that his unscheduled soaking had made his briefs almost totally irrelevant. They clung to him like a second skin, hiding nothing. She looked away knowing that the flush of blood surging through her body was no longer entirely down to the heat of the sauna.

He picked up a towel and wrapped it around his hips with a sigh. "It's my fault. I should have warned Maggie to keep you away from the sauna. You're so tired and run down you could just as easily have fainted from the heat."

"I'm not the fainting kind. Drowning's more my style," she managed a slight smile.

His answering grin wiped out the lines of worry that had settled around his eyes. "At least it hasn't affected your tongue. What were you trying to do, drum up some publicity for Greenlea's opening ceremony?"

She shook her head as she leaned back against the wall and closed her eyes. The heat was getting to her again now, drugging her into a cocoon of warm towels. If only Pierce would stop talking she might be able to sleep. The thought was suddenly very compelling and she had begun to drift away when he reached out and shook her.

"Kerry, for goodness sake! You can't sleep here," he groaned, pulling her to her feet. "Come on, concentrate for a bit longer until I get you to a day bed."

He pushed the door open as he spoke and led her through to the relaxation area. It was empty. She looked around dazedly.

"Is Maggie still sorting out her deliveries?"

"No. She's having a well-deserved coffee break," he stripped off her damp towels as he spoke and wrapped her in a long toweling robe as if she were a parcel to be posted, seemingly unaware of the intimacy of his actions.

"I offered to take over because we never leave the Spa unattended and besides I wanted a chance to talk to you uninterrupted." He tightened the sash at her waist and then kept hold of the ends and pulled her to him.

The inflection in his voice combined with the hardening of his body as he pressed against her made her heart jump. Things hadn't changed after all. He still wanted her, still loved her. Tentatively she wound her arms about his neck feeling the muscles across his shoulders ripple as he bent towards her, and when his mouth found hers, she was waiting.

His skin was hot from the sauna and his hair slicked into damp curls as she raked it with suddenly impatient fingers, her kisses wild from three years of hunger. Passion fizzed between them, fusing his mouth to hers as his tongue darted and danced across the line of her teeth before plunging deeper. Then he plucked at the sash he'd fastened so carefully a few moments earlier, and the touch of his hands on her bare skin drove her beyond the barriers of commonsense to the point where the sensations firing her body were the only reality. With a low cry she rubbed herself against him, her hardened nipples brushing the damp whorls of hair that covered his chest. With a sharp intake of breath he pushed the robe away from her shoulders and printed kisses on the soft curves of her skin.

She squeezed her eyes shut and concentrated on the pinpoints of fire that began to blaze across her body as his mouth travelled lower, the rasp of his cheek against the velvet softness of her breast creating a whole new range of sensations that set her fingers exploring an achingly familiar path.

With a sound that was half anger and half despair, Pierce scooped her up and pressed her tightly to him. Then he set her down on the day bed, pulled her robe together and covered her with towels.

"I must be totally mad! Why the hell do you always have this effect on me?" His face was flushed and furious as he reached for another robe from the pile beside the door and thrust his arms into its sleeves. He was only just in time. He was still knotting the sash when Maggie burst in through the door with a smile that quickly faded into embarrassed disbelief. Pierce took command of the situation with commendable mastery although Kerry could still hear the note of frustration in his voice.

"I've just been practicing my life saving skills because Kerry was doing a very good imitation of drowning when I found her."

It worked like a charm, instantly distracting Maggie from the tense atmosphere and turning her into a concerned professional. "Whatever happened? Did you faint or something?"

"I think she's just over-tired. She's been under a lot of strain recently," Pierce answered for Kerry as if she were a particularly dim-witted child. He sounded bored and disinterested now that he could hand her over and by the time he'd retrieved his wet clothes from the sauna Maggie was fussing over Kerry as if she were an invalid.

* * *

Kerry drifted in and out of sleep, listening to the sounds from the next room with a detached sense of reality. She could hear the monotonous undertone of the television news, the clink of a glass as someone poured a drink, and there were muffled voices too. Was one of them Pierce? She couldn't tell and anyway she didn't care, all she wanted to do was to sleep again. She rolled over and shut her eyes. The next time she woke up everything was silent.

She lay still for a long time, luxuriating in the fact that the knots of tension which had gripped her body for so long had been loosened by Maggie's massage. The darkness washed over her, tempting her to sleep again. This time she fought it, however, knowing she had to face what was happening to her while her mind was clear and she was relaxed. Turning her head towards the grey lozenge of window outlined against the blackness of the walls, she relived the moments she'd spent with Pierce in the Spa.

There was no mistake. They had been equally aroused. She blushed as she recalled her erotic reaction to his touch. It was all very well for him to excuse her by telling Maggie she was suffering from stress, but whatever he might believe, she could no longer hide the truth from herself. She still loved him. Worse, she still wanted him.

She rolled onto her side, her eyes staring into the darkness as she wondered how he really felt about her. Was it a shadow of the love they'd once shared that had prompted his passionate assault on her senses or was it just an overdose of testosterone? It had to be one or the other because she was under no illusions about her body. She had nothing left that would have turned him on. What had once been slenderness had long ago become angles as her curves diminished along with the bloom of her skin. Caring for the twins on a shoestring hadn't given her time to take care of her body.

She reached out and snapped on the bedside light and then pushed the bedcovers away. Her body had fined down almost to boyishness and a glance in the mirror opposite showed a cropped head and huge, waif-like eyes. There was nothing of the old Kerry Farrow left, nothing that could possibly attract Pierce, nothing that could compete with the voluptuous, athletic beauty of Marissa Reynolds.

She stared despondently at her reflection as she recalled Maggie's words. How was Marissa going to react when she found out about the twins and discovered Kerry was back in Pierce's life? Never a good loser, she would be bitchy and vindictive. She would make things hell for all of them. The thought made Kerry shudder with despair. How could Pierce do this? How could he possibly contemplate marrying her when she looked like this and when he was all but engaged to Marissa? Perhaps he intended to have the best of both worlds: his children and his mistress, with Kerry slotted in between as a necessary inconvenience, someone to be ignored once the wedding was over.

She groaned as she swung her feet to the floor. It was madness! She wouldn't go through with it. There had to be another way. Surely they could agree to share the children. She would promise him anything he wanted if only he would let Ben and Lauren stay with her without the travesty of a marriage. Those few moments alone with him in the Spa had shown her how painful it would be to live with him and love him while knowing all the time that deep down he resented her.

Hastily she pulled on the clothes that were folded neatly across the arm of a chair. The corduroy jeans had seen better days and the baggy sweater had once been bright pink before it faded to indeterminate beige from repeated washing. Neither of them was attractive but they had been the closest things to hand when Pierce had told her to pack sufficient clothes for a short stay at Greenleas.

"I'll take you home in time to see the children on Thursday evening," he'd promised. "But in the meantime you're staying with me so I can keep an eye on you."

One glance at the set expression on his face had dissuaded Kerry from argument and she had obediently fetched her clothes and then sobbed all over him in the van when they arrived at Greenleas. And somehow her tears and her acquiescence had had a softening effect on him, so he had restrained the worst of his impatience until that fateful moment in the Spa when an over active testosterone had got the better of him. What would have happened if Maggie hadn't burst in on them she would never know. She did know he was irritated with her though because he hadn't tried to hide it when Maggie eventually delivered her to his suite. Nor had he made any reference to what had happened between them in the Spa. Instead he'd merely asked her if she was hungry, ordered a meal that she only picked at, and then left her quite alone.

She smoothed her sweater over her hips and combed her fingers through her hair. That would have to do. Nobody was going to see her anyway, not at this time of night. She collected her scuffed leather tote from the bedside table and her trainers from beneath the bed. Then she tiptoed to the door and pushed down the handle. She would go and see Mel. Trying to sort out her thoughts on her own wasn't working but maybe talking them through with someone would. Pierce had thrown the keys to the van onto the kitchen counter when they arrived at Greenleas so unless he'd moved them, getting there was no longer a problem, nor was disturbing her friend in the middle of the night. Nothing fazed Mel. She was exactly the person Kerry needed and she was going to see her even if she had to walk every step of the way.

She gave a scream of fright as the door handle jerked under her fingers and then she jumped backwards as the door crashed open revealing Pierce, clad in a loosely tied silk dressing gown and a scarlet rage.

"And where exactly do you think you're going?" He advanced menacingly until she was backed up against the bed. "What do you want me to do Kerry? Tie you down until Saturday?"

For the first time she was frightened. She had never seen him like this before, never heard the snarl of rage in his voice. He'd often been angry, with her, with himself, with his tennis opponents, but this was something darker. She started quaking inside but it didn't show in the lift of her chin.

"You can do what you like but I won't marry you. It isn't fair to either of us or to the children."

Chapter Six

"I didn't realize fairness had a place in your life," Pierce's voice cut through her explanation like a knife. "After all there was nothing very fair about bringing two children into the world and then depriving them of their inalienable right to a mother and a father as well as a stable home."

"There will be nothing stable about a home continually tormented with arguments," Kerry snapped, the edge of guilt his words prompted tipping her into an answering anger. "Leave them with me Pierce and visit us sometimes. I don't want you disrupting our lives."

At her words the high color faded from his face leaving it sallow and drawn and when he answered her, his voice was clipped and cold.

"I've already told you they belong here at Greenleas, with both their parents, not shut into a shabby house with a mother who is too tired to care for them properly and a father whose visits would apparently disrupt their routine. Make your choice now Kerry. Are you coming too, as my wife, or do Ben and Lauren come alone? And before you answer make no mistake about it, you come on my terms or not at all."

"Which are?" Although her heart was pounding and her throat was dry, Kerry kept her head high.

"That we work together. As far as the children are concerned we will present a united front. We will be the parents they deserve. I don't want to continually fight you over them. I want to give you the chance to be a proper mother, not someone who is too worn out to think straight, but I'm not going to let you do it at my expense. You owe it to me to cooperate while I catch up on the two years I've spent without them."

He paused and gave her a tight little smile. "I'm under no illusions Kerry. One word from you could reduce me to a bogeyman status that would keep Lauren, at least, beyond my reach for the next five years."

"I can't believe you'd think I'd do that to you. I...well...it's..." Kerry was lost for words as her anger faded to incredulity.

He sighed. "I don't know what to think anymore. Once I thought I knew exactly who you were but you proved me wrong when you cut out on me so now I'm finding it difficult to give you a second chance, particularly when you keep throwing it back in my face. Where on earth were you going at this time of night?"

"I wasn't running away if that's what you think...I was going to see Mel. I...I was going to tell her everything." She dropped her tote onto the rumpled sheets and walked across to the window so he wouldn't see the despair in her eyes. Behind her, Pierce slumped onto the edge of the bed and ran agitated fingers through his hair; unaware she could see his reflection in the glass. His action touched her as nothing else had done, showing her his hidden vulnerability as he fought for his children.

She knew he was right too. Her decision to hide Ben and Lauren from him had been the wrong one, even though she'd made it for all the right reasons, so now she owed Ben and Lauren a chance of a real family life. That marriage was part of the deal was something she would have to accept if she wanted to keep her children. She would only do it if he would agree to her terms though.

"I have a stipulation of my own," she turned around abruptly and leaned against the windowsill, hoping he wouldn't notice how her hands were still shaking. "I'll marry you and encourage the children to accept you. I accept I owe you all of that. But I'll only do it if you agree to give me space to breath. I want to be my own person as well as Mrs Pierce Simon."

"I thought that was a given," he sat upright, the momentary strain banished from his face by the rigid self-discipline he'd learned early in his career. "You were there when Mel and I discussed details even if you weren't in a fit state to join in. You know what arrangements we've made for Melanie's Kitchen. Marrying me is not going to interfere with that part of your life Kerry. It's going to enhance it."

114

"I wasn't referring to my job. I was referring to our...personal relationship," she spoke slowly and deliberately, anxious he should understand now, before it was too late.

He grinned at her, a trace of the old Pierce flashing through his weariness "If you mean the one behind bedroom doors, you didn't used to be so delicate."

"Maybe not," she blushed faintly and shrugged. "But it doesn't alter the facts. I'm not going to sleep with you Pierce. I'll be your wife...but in name only."

She wasn't sure what she had been expecting; anger, impatience, laughter, even ridicule, but the one thing she hadn't anticipated was the expression of relief that washed across his face. It went as quickly as it came, leaving her unsure if she'd read him correctly as he pushed himself up from the bed with a disinterested shrug.

"As you wish, even if you do seem to have changed your tune somewhat from earlier today. As far as I'm concerned you can do whatever you like as long as Ben and Lauren don't suffer. Now for goodness sake go back to bed so we can finish the night in peace because tomorrow's going to be another long, busy day."

He went then, leaving her staring after him in disbelief. Although she'd meant what she said, knowing she couldn't ever share him with Marissa or any other woman who came into his life, and so preferring to do without him entirely, she hadn't expected him to accept her terms so readily. What she'd wanted was to fight him, to force him to agree against his will. She had wanted to prove to herself that the brief surge of desire he'd shown in the Spa was more than just an old memory rekindled. Well he'd very effectively destroyed that dream. It was obvious he didn't want her at all. Worse, he was relieved she didn't want to sleep with him.

It brought home to her more than anything else that he was marrying her for the children, so although she climbed obediently back into bed she didn't close her eyes again.

* * *

"Hi," Mel pushed open the door and walked into the kitchen where Kerry was dejectedly buttering a slice of toast. She had deliberately stayed in bed until she heard Pierce leave, not wanting to see him again until she had to. Now, after a hot shower, she was preparing a breakfast that she wasn't going to eat.

"Mel!" She greeted her friend with a gasp of relief. "Have you come to wrestle the lists away from Pierce and take over Melanie's Kitchen again?"

"Not on your life," Mel laughed. "I'm too busy enjoying the break before he sets us to work. No! I've come to take you in hand. Boss's orders."

"I didn't know I needed taking in hand," Kerry managed a smile as she pushed another

116

slice of bread into the toaster and spooned coffee granules into two mugs.

"Have you looked in your wardrobe recently Kerry because I have, and unless you're going to get married in jeans and a sweater then you need help, fast. Now pass the butter will you because I've finally got my appetite back."

She spread butter and marmalade liberally on a slice of toast and then bit off a large mouthful. She eyed Kerry thoughtfully while she chewed it. "Haven't you got anything to say? Most brides are either over-excited or full of pre-wedding nerves this close to their wedding."

"Sorry to disappoint you. I'll try to do better tomorrow," Kerry sipped her coffee, using the mug as a barrier to hide behind.

"Well at least tell me something about your past. How you met Pierce and all that stuff. Really Kerry, you're such a dark horse. I wouldn't be keeping quiet about someone as gorgeous as Pierce Simon.

"There's nothing to tell," Kerry stood up and began stacking the empty plates and mugs. "We had a bit of a fling a long time ago and then he came back into my life by chance on Monday. You know the rest."

"How can you be so matter-of-fact about it all?" Mel wailed. "With someone like Pierce wanting to marry you so badly that he's not even prepared to wait in case you slip through his fingers again, you should be walking on air. I know Mum and Dad are. At first they were worried you were making a rash decision for all he wrong reasons, but now they know you've known him for ages they're really pleased for you. Apart from the fact that Pierce obviously loves you to bits, it solves everything else as well: your job, your financial problems, even Ben and Lauren. By this time next week they'll be calling him daddy and will probably have forgotten what life was like before he came along."

"I guess," Kerry carried the dishes over to the kitchen counter, keeping her back turned while she attempted to get a grip of herself. Last night's argument with Pierce had shown her how futile it would be to discuss things with Mel and ask for her advice because he had made the fact she had no choice very clear. Either she married him and kept the children or she lost everything. So somehow she had to dredge up enough enthusiasm to make her friend believe she was glad she was getting married. She couldn't spoil the small amount of excitement she was bringing to Mel and her parents, not when they had all done so much for her. She didn't want to worry them either, so with a big effort she turned around and gave her friend a bright smile.

"What's all this about taking me in hand then?"

"As I said, boss's orders," Mel pushed back her chair and stood up. "We're going on a shopping spree because you don't have a single dress in your wardrobe. You don't even have a skirt if you discount that black polyester thing you wear whenever you have to serve food."

Kerry gave her a startled look as she mentally reviewed the contents of her wardrobe. Mel was right. She owned nothing by jeans and trousers plus a few T-shirts and sweaters. Shut in with the twins she had little use for anything else. Her friend gave a crow of laughter when she saw the expression on her face.

"I'm right aren't I? And you haven't even thought about what you're going to wear when you get married have you? Really Kerry you are the limit. It's time you started thinking about yourself now Ben and Lauren are growing up. You'd be quite pretty if you ditched that unisex image and grew your hair."

The twinkle in her friend's eyes forced a smile from Kerry as she made for the door. "Thanks for the vote of confidence! If I need so much help I guess I'd better let you do your worst. I'll put myself in your hands for the rest of the day if that's what it takes to keep you and Pierce happy."

Mel didn't need any further prompting. Within minutes they were driving out of the car park in George's elderly but immaculate Rover. "Dad lent me this because Pierce needed the van. You'd better feel properly honored Kerry because it's his pride and joy."

"I am...I do," Kerry settled into the passenger seat with a sigh. Everyone was being so kind. Mel, George and Mary were treating her like real family. They were so excited and pleased for what they saw as her good fortune so the least she could do was be grateful and not spoil things for them.

* * *

By the end of the afternoon the old Rover was laden down with parcels. Boxes and carrier bags littered the back seat and there were more in the trunk. They were both tired but Mel, at least, was satisfied. Parking outside her parent's house she chatted happily as they carried the results of their shopping expedition indoors.

"You do realize I'm now on the lookout for a rich husband. Today has given me a taste for money."

Kerry forced a smile. "If that's what you want then you'll snap one up in no time at Greenleas. A club like that attracts wealthy men like ducks to water."

It was all surface chatter, a continuation of the banter they'd indulged in all day. Kerry had started it once she'd accepted she couldn't tell her friend the truth about her relationship with Pierce. She had only faltered once and that was when she discovered Pierce was footing the bill. Until then she had thought Mel was giving her a wage advance and because of this, and because after three years of hardship, thrift was ingrained into her, she marched into the nearest chain store and started sorting through a rack of dresses being sold at a reduced price.

"What do you think you're doing?" Mel hurried in after her and seized her arm. "Pierce said to try Chantal's first and then go on to First Edition although I can't imagine how he knows about such things."

"Pierce?" Kerry stared at her, hoping she'd heard wrong, but Mel just gave an excited nod.

"Yes Pierce. He said to spend whatever it takes. We just have to tell the sales assistants to send the bill to Greenleas."

"But…I thought it was you…I thought you were giving me an advance on my wages."

Mel laughed out loud. "If I could afford to give you the sort of advance you need to buy something at Chantal's, then I wouldn't be running Melanie's Kitchen. Come on Kerry. Pierce wants to do this for you so lighten up a bit. It's going to be fun."

Seething underneath, Kerry followed her out of the shop. The state of her wardrobe had nothing to do with Pierce, nor did the sort of clothes she intended to buy. How dare he tell Mel where to shop! She wasn't about to let him recreate the old Kerry Farrow whatever Mel said. Remembering how he used to look at her when she wore something tight or revealing, she decided to only choose things that covered her from her neck to her ankles.

Then she saw the excitement on Mel's face and, swallowing her resentment, she shrugged. After all, what were a few clothes to him? She could remember when he'd bought a dozen shirts at a time, or spent several thousand pounds on a watch he didn't need, so if he wanted to buy his future wife some clothes, he could. She apologized for her initial lack of enthusiasm and threw herself into the fiasco that was her wedding trousseau with every outward indication of enjoyment. The effort took its toll though and she stacked the pile of packages in the hallway with a sigh.

"Mummy!" The whirlwind that was Ben rushed into the hallway and interrupted her thoughts by hurling himself at her legs. "Lookit Pierce gived me!"

He waved a plump wrist in the air and then attempted to find handholds in her jeans and sweater. She laughed as she swung him upwards, burying her face in the soft baby smell of his neck and planting a kiss just beneath his ear. He wriggled free with a frown.

"No! Lookit watch."

He thrust his arm under her nose and proudly displayed a sturdy plastic watch with both an analogue and a digital display. It had a bright orange button as well, and when he pressed it a very noisy alarm sounded next to her ear.

"Goodness me that's loud!" She pretended he'd deafened her and kept on smiling until Pierce strolled out from the sitting room holding Lauren's hand. When she saw him her look was pure venom. So that's why he'd sent her out with Mel, so he could spend time alone with the children using presents to buy their affection. And he'd pushed his way into George and

Mary's house too. How dare he manipulate her like this! And how dare he push his way into her friends' lives without a by your leave from her.

"Hello, had a good day?" He included Mel in the question, a slight frown his only indication that he'd noticed Kerry's reaction.

"Yes thank you." She knew her reply was far too stiff and unfriendly for someone greeting her future husband and that she should try harder for appearance's sake but she couldn't do it. Instead she bent to give Lauren a kiss before he could say anything else.

"You too," she said as her daughter held up a watch with a bright blue button. Then she hugged her close. Lauren flung her arms around her mother's neck and held on tight. "Mummy stay here."

"Yes darling, Mummy's staying," Kerry picked her up, feeling guilty she had left the children with George and Mary for so long. It wouldn't matter so much if they were used to being part of a family but with only Kerry as their base, they needed extra security. It was something she struggled with when it manifested itself in Lauren's tendency to cling and Ben's possessiveness.

* * *

The next hour was taken up with the children's supper and while Ben and Lauren scooped pasta into mouths ringed with tomato sauce, Mary gave everyone a blow-by-blow account of everything they'd done during the day. Eventually, her eyes glazing over, Mel interrupted.

"You've held court for long enough Mum. Don't you want to see what we've bought?"

"Of course I do dear," Mary looked slightly abashed as she met Kerry's eyes. Instantly Kerry knew what was wrong. Mary's incessant chatter was a symptom of an uncharacteristic nervousness. She was waiting for Kerry to tell everyone what she had already guessed.

Kerry frowned as she looked across at Pierce. They were in this together so the least he could do was to be there for her, but he was too busy talking to George to notice that anything was amiss. Mel was oblivious too. She was far too occupied with the result of their shopping spree. Unfolding carefully wrapped tissue paper she held up a pale blue dress.

"Look, isn't this gorgeous? And it's just right for Kerry's coloring." She turned to Pierce with an expression of immense satisfaction. "I took you at your word you know. We've spent a fortune."

He smiled. "With or without Kerry's cooperation?"

"Mostly with," Mel chuckled. "At first I thought she was going to be difficult but after the first couple of hours she cut it down to the occasional protest. She could learn to spend money yet!"

"Is that meant to be good news?" The amused glint in Pierce's eyes was a reminder to

Kerry of her original lifestyle and she broke in hurriedly before he was tempted to enlarge on her past.

"There seems to have been an awful lot of discussion going on behind my back. Is there anything else I should know?"

Pierce gave her a level gaze as he saw through her ploy. "Only that I've been invited to dinner. I think George intends to put me through the third degree to check that I'm good enough for you."

"Damn right Sir!" George gave a delighted chuckle as he heaved himself up from his chair with only a small wince as pain shot through his arthritic knee. "That's why I phoned you and invited you to join us. Kerry's too much a part of the family for me to give her away to just anyone, isn't that right Mary?"

"Mmm…" Mary's eyes were on Kerry. "I don't think we need to worry about Pierce though. He has all the necessary qualifications…"

She left the sentence unfinished, turned away abruptly and busied herself wiping the smears of sauce from the children's faces. The others looked puzzled. Mel turned to Kerry.

"Does she know something we don't?"

"Yes…that Pierce is Ben and Lauren's father." Kerry stood up and clutched the back of her chair as she spoke. Her face was flushed and defiant and her voice was too loud as she watched the effect her words had on George and Mel and saw their disbelief fade into confusion.

125

"Don't upset yourself my dear. It's better out," Mary's comforting hand on her shoulder was the last straw and she burst into tears.

* * *

"I knew the moment I saw Pierce standing on the doorstep," Mary accepted a glass of wine from her husband with a self-satisfied smile. She raised it in a toast to where Kerry was standing beside Pierce, trying to look as if she was enjoying the weight of his arm across her shoulders.

At Mel's insistence she had changed into one of her new outfits although she had balked at anything dressier than a midnight blue sweater and a pair of designer jeans. Casual but elegant, the dark blue flattered her coloring at the same time that it detracted from the slight puffiness around her eyes. She smiled as Mel and George joined in, glad they would never know the whole truth of her marriage to Pierce.

Following her abrupt announcement Pierce had taken charge of the twins and left her to make her peace with her friends, murmuring that everyone would be able to talk more freely without him there. The move had impressed George and he'd said so with great feeling as he turned to Kerry and demanded she tell them everything. And she had told them everything that mattered, even explaining some of her reasons for keeping Pierce in ignorance about Ben and Lauren.

"I didn't think it was fair to burden him when he was at the peak of his career and had already told me he didn't want children," she said.

"You should still have given him the choice," Mary shook her head decisively. "Think what a shock it's been for him to discover he has a family. You're lucky he wants to marry you and look after Ben and Lauren. A lot of men might not have been so forgiving."

George, who had barely spoken since Kerry's announcement, shook his head. "Where does love come in all this Kerry? You and Pierce have both talked to us about the importance of a home for the children, and you've told us why you left him too. But neither of you has mentioned love. Are you just marrying him for the sake of the children? And what about Pierce? If he didn't want a family three years ago, why would he want one now? Have you really thought this through my dear because in this day and age being a single mother is nothing to be ashamed about? Couldn't you both wait a while... just long enough to be sure of one another?"

That was when Mel, who was still shaking her head over Kerry's confession, jumped up from her chair and took charge. "Dad, all that's in the past now. Pierce has asked Kerry to marry him and she's accepted. She could have said no but she didn't so we need to congratulate her not give her the third degree. I propose we celebrate the fact that they've found one another again and want to make a new life together, not question it. Come on Kerry, into the bedroom with you. Those jeans and the sweater look good but they don't fit the occasion. It's time you put on some real glad rags so we can celebrate properly.

They'd all laughed at that and then Mary had bustled out of the room to help Pierce with the children while George took himself off to buy a bottle of champagne. He'd arrived back just in time to see Kerry leaving the spare bedroom wearing a pale blue dress. He gave her an admiring look.

"You've got legs then!"

When she giggled nervously he gave her a hug.

"No regrets Kerry? I don't want to put a damper on the occasion but you are sure you're doing the right thing aren't you, because we're on your side you know. Marriage isn't always the right answer even though he does seem like a nice chap."

"I am sure George but thank you anyway," she hugged him back; very glad he would never know about the threats Pierce had used to get her this far.

Pierce joined them then, the expression on his face leaving Kerry in no doubt he'd heard everything.

"Ben and Lauren want to say goodnight," he held out his hand. She took it without a word and let him lead her into the bedroom where the twins, drooping with sleep, were lying on their

128

pillows waiting for her. Mary was there too but as soon as she'd finished folding the children's clothes she left the room, closing the door quietly behind her.

"Mummy pretty," Lauren put out a questioning finger and touched the large shiny buttons on Kerry's dress. Then she pressed her hot little palm to Kerry's lips. It was a signal for her mother to kiss first her hand, then her wrist, and then smother her with kisses until she was writhing and giggling with delight. Pierce watched, smiling, until Kerry started to get up from the bed. When Lauren realized the game was over she shrieked for more. Her excitement encouraged Ben to join in and soon the whole thing got out of hand as both children clung to Kerry's neck, their voices shrill and demanding.

"That's enough," Pierce stepped in and removed them gently but firmly, inserting each small body back under the covers. "Mummy's tired and so are you. There will be plenty of time for games tomorrow."

Lauren gave in, sticking her thumb in her mouth with a final giggle, but Ben wriggled around until he was sitting upright again. He glared at his father with a mutinous expression on his face. Pierce held his ground while Kerry looked on in trepidation, waiting for an eruption of temper that didn't come. An unexpected smile crept across her face as she watched Pierce match his son look for look. Maybe there would be a few benefits in having him around after all.

He saw her smile and grinned. "You can only deal with it if you recognize it."

"You mean you were like that?" She watched Ben collapse onto his pillow and start to suck his thumb with something close to incredulity.

"Still am," he turned out the overhead light and put his arm around her as she stood looking down at the children. "It's the same trait that's seen me across the tennis courts of the world and that's driving me to develop Greenleas into an international centre. I'm always trying to prove myself, to stop anyone else getting the upper hand."

"But surely that's very different from the tennis circuit?" She asked the question with genuine interest.

"Not so much. There's not as much personal support of course and there's nobody to cosset me or put up with the bursts of temperament I used to display on the circuit. I still work with a team though, only this time Greenleas is the focus of attention whereas in the past everyone concentrated on me and my tennis."

"Has the transition been easy?"

He grinned at her. "Not really but when it gets me down I play god. Getting dictatorial with the people around me salves my hurt pride." Although the room was only lit by the dim glow of the night-light she could still see the twinkle in his eyes. It told her he knew exactly what was said about him at Greenleas and even suspected Maggie might have told her.

She dimpled at his unexpected honesty but then she remembered her own circumstances and turned away, her voice bitter. "That's something you don't need to tell me. I'm experiencing it at first hand in case you haven't noticed!"

He stopped her with a tug of his hand. "Don't hate me for forcing you into this Kerry. I promise you it'll work if you just give it a chance."

Their eyes met and held, and for a brief moment she glimpsed something almost pleading in his expression, but then Mel called to say the meal was ready. Immediately she pulled away from him, not wanting to see anything that might make her feel sorry for him because, if she did, she would have something else to add to her burden of guilt.

* * *

The rest of the evening went well, with Pierce and Mel putting themselves out to entertain, even vying for attention because they were both extroverts who enjoyed an audience as much as they enjoyed a joke at their own expense. By the time Pierce left he seemed to have been part of the family for years. Even Kerry, with Saturday hanging over her like the sword of Damocles, found she had enjoyed the evening sufficiently to smile at him as she accompanied him to the door.

Her smile fell on stony ground, however, because once they were alone his good humor fell away like a discarded coat. He opened the front door. "See me to the car."

The softness in his voice was for Mel's benefit as she whisked past them on her way to the kitchen with the dirty coffee cups. Kerry followed him wordlessly, trailing him down the path like a shadow in the moonlight until they reached the gate. Then he turned and, with a glance back at the house, deliberately bent his head and kissed her. His mouth was harsh and with a gasp she tried to draw away from him but he was too strong. He cradled her head in his hand and forced her lips apart with a bruising anger that left her shaken and afraid.

"That was for the benefit of your supporter's club. I'd hate them to think your silence this evening means you have some doubts about marrying me."

She hit out at him then, too angry to care about choosing her words. "I haven't married you yet and if this is how you intend to treat me then I'm not going to."

He caught her flailing arms effortlessly and trapped them between their bodies, pulling her close. His hands felt like iron bands on her back and his eyes were like chips of black ice. "Oh but you will my love, and unlike this evening, you'll look as if you're enjoying every minute of it, if only for Ben and Lauren's sake."

The threat was unmistakable. His good humor throughout the evening, his generosity, even the affection he had displayed earlier, it was all an act to gain credibility with the people who mattered to Kerry.

The anger drained out of her as she stared up at him. She didn't even bother to move when he finally released her. "Why do you want to marry me Pierce, when nothing I do pleases you? When you can see how unhappy it's making me. Why don't you just fight me for the children?"

"Because it would take too long," he stood with his hand on the gate, his expression grim under the wavering streetlight. "I don't intend to lose another second of their lives while lawyers earn a fortune through court proceedings and appeals. Ben and Lauren belong to both of us Kerry. I was just as active in their creation as you were, something I remember with a certain degree of pleasure, even if you don't."

His eyes grew darker as he leaned towards her and locked his hands around her waist, pulling her against the gate so that the wrought iron bit into her thighs and the soft flesh of her stomach. "Make no mistake about it. I've already got the special license and the rings so you'll marry me on Saturday and you'll smile as you do it."

Chapter Seven

Smiling was the last thing Kerry felt like doing when she arrived at the registry office on Saturday morning and saw Pierce. Unfamiliar in a dark suit and tie, he came over to where she was standing with Mel and George and deliberately kissed her on the lips with every appearance of pleasure. She stiffened and then remained poker straight when he slipped his arm around her waist.

"Pre-wedding nerves?" he asked Mel with believable innocence. She nodded her agreement.

"We've hardly managed to get a word out of her this morning. Even Ben and Lauren gave up and went off with Mum to do some shopping."

"They are coming though," this time Pierce addressed Kerry, his eyes full of fury although his lips were still smiling.

"Afterwards," she replied through tight lips. "They chatter too much to risk having them around during the ceremony, so Mary has promised to meet us outside afterwards."

She felt an inward surge of triumph as he accepted her decision with a slight frown, glad she'd managed to score a point by keeping the children away from the wedding. She knew her reasons were sound. Knew there was a distinct possibility Ben would grow bored and create a noisy diversion or that Lauren would ask too many questions in her penetrating treble voice. She also knew that a registry office wedding was far less formal than a church service so any problems could have been dealt with. Indeed, Mary had been prepared to try, but Kerry had remained adamant. Illogical as it was she felt that if the children were actually present when she married Pierce, they would have some weakening effect on her resolve to stop loving him.

She looked at him now and wished emotions could be made to follow a set path but it was quite hopeless. The proud angle of his dusky profile, brooding now because Ben and Lauren were going to miss the ceremony, was almost enough to break her. It was one thing to tell herself he was a heartless bully who would go to any lengths to get his children, and quite another to stop her heart thudding against her breast when he gave her that blue sideways glance.

"Okay?" he didn't smile.

She nodded, clutched the small posy of pink rosebuds Mel had insisted on ordering, and walked with him into the building. George and Mel followed, their faces wreathed in smiles of sympathy at what they thought were pre-wedding nerves, instead of the shriek of her breaking heart.

* * *

It was over in minutes. A few words from the registrar, her own promise little more than a whisper, Pierce's voice deep and sure, and then a heavy gold band was pushed gently over her finger. Several signatures later she was Mrs Pierce Simon. Such little acts for something so momentous, something she would have embraced with all her heart three years earlier but which now left her feeling full of despair.

"Congratulations!" Mel hugged her and then grinned at Pierce. "Doesn't the bridegroom usually kiss the bride?"

He obliged with a smile, his lips descending swiftly before Kerry could turn her cheek. And this time it was different. There was no animosity in his kiss, only a lingering sweetness as his mouth brushed hers and his arm tightened possessively about her waist.

Surprised, she neither drew away nor responded but, instead, stood locked in his arms like a marble statue and almost as pale. He lifted his head and frowned, assessing the faint shadows under her eyes and her unnatural pallor.

"Are you feeling all right?"

She nodded wordlessly because she supposed that to be alive and not in actual physical pain counted as being all right. Maybe she was as right as she was ever going to be again. Cautiously she fingered the heavy wedding ring, twisting it around with her thumb and forefinger. It felt like a manacle, anchoring her to this man who didn't want her, and who was only looking at her like this because George and Mel were watching.

* * *

Mary and the children were waiting outside. Mary was armed with confetti and the twins were each clutching a lucky charm. Ben saw them first and charged across the wintry grass with his arms outstretched.

"Cat!" he shouted. "Black cat!"

Pierce caught him with a chuckle and hoisted him skywards. "I think you're meant to give that to Mummy?"

Obligingly Ben handed Kerry a small wooden cat with several white ribbons around its neck. Then he look round for his sister. She was still holding Mary's hand but was wriggling frantically in an attempt to get away. Kerry waved and then, disregarding the rough gravelly path, she went down on her knees as Lauren finally broke free and came running towards her. She was giggling excitedly as she trailed a lucky silver horseshoe behind her.

"Mary gived," she explained, handing it to Kerry. Then her eyes brightened. "Pretty flowers!"

"Yes, they are very pretty flowers," Kerry agreed, smiling her thanks to Mary as she let Lauren hold the posy.

"Mummy pretty too," Lauren abandoned the flowers when she noticed Kerry's rose pink dress and shoes with heels. Only used to seeing her mother in jeans she looked slightly alarmed.

"She is isn't she," Pierce, still holding Ben, descended to Lauren's level and put out one brown finger to smooth his daughter's curls. She smiled, still slightly in awe of him but prepared to be friendly.

"Don't move," they hadn't noticed George circling them with a camera and they all looked up startled as he addressed them. He grinned. "Come on, smile all of you. This is a wedding remember, so I want a happy family group."

He took a lot of photographs after that. Kerry alone, Kerry and Pierce together, the twins in various combinations and then some that included Mel and Mary. Finally, at Pierce's insistence, there were a few of all of them thanks to an obliging bystander who followed George's anxious instructions and clicked away obediently. And because everyone was pleased, and because the children chuckled with delight every time George told them to say cheese, and because Mary kept wiping tears of happiness from her eyes, Kerry smiled in every one of them even though her heart was breaking.

* * *

They ate at a discreet restaurant not far from the registry office. Pierce had booked a table in a private room where Ben and Lauren couldn't disgrace themselves. The manager greeted Pierce like an old friend and bowed low over Kerry's hand when she was introduced as his wife.

"It's a great pleasure to meet you Madame," he said as he led her to the table and pulled out a chair. "I will do my best to make this meal a memorable one."

And he was as good as his word. After pouring everyone a glass of champagne he gave them plenty of time to look at the menu and then waited patiently while they made their choice. Everything was beautifully cooked and presented and the red and white wines that accompanied the different courses were excellent, but Kerry couldn't eat. She toyed with the food on her plate while the others chatted, and refused to look at Pierce. Instead she concentrated on the twins who were eating something far less exotic with great gusto.

"It seems to be a success," finally Pierce leaned across and touched her hand, smiling as he nodded towards the children's rapidly emptying plates.

She forced an answering smile. "The regular menu would have been wasted on them."

"That's what Carlo said. He offered to cook something that would keep them happy while we celebrated."

She stared at him and then asked the question that had been bugging her. "Why have you told him about our wedding when you quite obviously haven't told anyone else? Why didn't you invite a single guest Pierce? And what about your parents…when are you going to tell them?"

His fingers tightened on hers. "For goodness sake Kerry, have some sense! Apart from the fact that my parents are holidaying in Florida at the moment, what else could I do? I haven't been away from the circuit for long enough to lose my newsworthiness, especially as I've been promoting Greenleas on TV recently. I didn't think you'd be too keen to expose Ben and Lauren to the sort of hysterical media coverage we could have expected if news of our wedding leaked out either."

There was an edge of impatience in his voice that contradicted the expression in his eyes as he looked at her. For a moment she almost believed he was pleading with her, willing her to understand something he hadn't put into words. She looked down at their linked hands; his large and brown against her small, work roughened one.

"I'm sorry. You're right. I guess I'm not really thinking straight at the moment."

He ran his forefinger across a red burn mark on her thumb as he gave a faint sigh. "I'm sorry too, for bludgeoning you into all of this. I know you hate me for it but I'll try not to make it too difficult for you. And once word gets out about Ben and Lauren you'll be glad we're married, glad of the protection I can give all three of you."

She stared at him, suddenly realizing what he'd saved her from by insisting they marry quickly. Another week, a casual word passed on, and their wedding would have been a circus with photographers and journalists descending like vultures. The whole story of their past relationship including her pregnancy, the birth of the twins, and the two years she had spent as a single parent, would have been splashed across the news in vivid detail. She shuddered.

He read her thoughts and squeezed her hand sympathetically before lifting it to his lips. "It hasn't happened. Nobody knows we're married apart from Mel and her parents, and Carlo, and he's the soul of discretion. And although I haven't said a thing to the people at Greenleas, there's a rumor going around that you're a relative who's just visiting. I don't know who started it but I'm not about to contradict it at the moment. Eventually we'll become public knowledge though and you'll have to be strong then."

She watched as his lips brushed her fingertips, mesmerized by the blue depths of his eyes and wishing she could believe the expression in them. If only his soft voice and public show of affection was more than just an act for the others.

"That's enough whispering you two," Mel broke into their conversation with a knowing grin. "You'll have time enough later for all the billing and cooing. In the meantime you've a cake to cut and champagne to drink."

It broke the mood and Pierce released Kerry's hand as they both admired the extravagant pink and white sugar confection Carlo placed in the centre of the table. Then he turned back to her with a smile.

"I imagine we're expected to do the honors while George wields his camera."

George grinned. He was already in position and he started clicking away as they pushed the knife into the icing. It sliced smoothly into a feather light sponge. Ben and Lauren clapped their hands in delight when they were handed small pieces on tiny pink plates.

"More! More!" Ben stuffed a great quantity into his mouth and then thrust his plate back in Pierce's direction.

"More cake please," his father cut another sliver but then held it just out of reach while Ben gave him a baleful glare, his bottom lip beginning to quiver with temper.

"He'll make a fuss," Kerry pleaded, not wanting to spoil the meal.

"Let him," Pierce shrugged as he turned back to his own plate without another glance in Ben's direction.

The others held their breath, knowing only too well the ear splitting shrieks he was capable of producing. Pierce smiled at them. "Surely you haven't finished. Mary, let Carlo pour you some more champagne."

She shook her head as she hastily scooped up a pink sugar flower and held it out to Ben, hoping to dispel the storm clouds that were gathering ominously about his knotted black eyebrows. Pierce, however, intercepted her and placed it next to the slice of cake on Ben's out-of-reach plate.

"Cake please," Ben's voice was very clear. In the stunned silence that followed his smile was cherubic. His father silently handed him the plate. Nobody said a word but Kerry had to blink hard as she watched her son chew his way through his second slice of cake. If she'd had any doubts about the wisdom of marrying Pierce for the sake of the children, his quiet authority with Ben had laid them to rest. They needed him.

She gave him a faint smile as their eyes met. He winked at her and then lifted his glass and proposed a toast to Mary, George and Mel for all they had done for his family. They responded with indignant protests and an insistence that the toasts should be reserved for the bride and groom. Watching Pierce charm them yet again, Kerry gave an inward sigh as she hoped he would never realize how much she needed him too.

* * *

The day dwindled to ordinary after the wedding breakfast, with George and Mary taking Ben and Lauren off for a brisk wintry

143

visit to the park while Mel, Pierce and Kerry returned to Greenleas: Mel to meet the kitchen staff and generally acquaint herself with the catering set up, Pierce to spend a couple of hours in his office, and Kerry to sort out the children's belongings before their bedtime.

Mary had suggested they should let Ben and Lauren stay with her for a few more days so Pierce and Kerry could enjoy a brief honeymoon, but Kerry had quickly scotched the idea by saying that it would be better for the children to get used to their father straight away.

"They need to be with us now," she said. "I don't want them to think Pierce is someone who is going to keep taking me away from them so it would be better if we all had a family holiday once they're used to their new home."

As she spoke she tried hard to ignore the glint in Pierce's eyes. She didn't want to know whether he was laughing at her, or whether he was irritated. All she wanted was to ensure she wouldn't have to spend any time alone with him.

* * *

Now, watching her children sleeping peacefully amongst their familiar collection of soft toys and teddy bears, she suddenly realized that for all her planning, she was still alone with Pierce. Once Ben and Lauren were asleep they rarely woke up, which meant she had to spend the rest of the evening in his company

144

pretending everything was fine. And it was fine as far as the twins were concerned.

They had inspected their new bedroom with interest and then squealed with delight when they discovered Pierce's bath made bubbles. Never having seen a Jacuzzi before they were as fascinated by the air inlets as with the frothy bubbles that crept up their stomachs and which Kerry dabbed onto their noses. Then, worn out by their busy day they had climbed into bed without a murmur, with only Lauren pausing to check that Kerry wasn't going anywhere. Used to a nursery and to frequent visits to George and Mary, as well as to Mel's house, they had no particular attachment to their own home. As long as Kerry was nearby and they had some familiar toys to play with, they were content anywhere. She sighed. She was the one with the difficulty.

She suffered every time Pierce brushed past her, every time that intense blue gaze rested on her. Thank goodness she'd resisted any sort of holiday and told Pierce she was going to help Mel move Melanie's Kitchen into the sports complex as soon as possible. Once she could concentrate on that she would be too busy to think during the day. At night she would say she was tired and go to bed early.

"What a shame they have to wake up," Pierce made her jump as he came up behind her.

"Regretting it already?" She responded to the humor in his voice with a tired smile.

145

He grinned. "Not as much as I regret the agreement we made."

Panic leapt into her throat and she swallowed nervously. "Pierce, you promised!"

"Did I? Did I actually say I promise never to make love to you Kerry?"

"No, but…"

"I thought not. Well you'll just have to hope I'm honorable then won't you, especially in view of our sleeping arrangements."

"What sleeping arrangements?" Until now Kerry had been too busy sorting out the twin's room to give a thought to where she was going to sleep.

"Well…I asked my manager to reorganize the beds so there would be room for Ben and Lauren. Unfortunately he can't have been listening properly because he, or whoever he asked to do it, has messed things up a bit I'm afraid."

He took her hand and led her out into the passageway that bisected the apartment, and then into the next bedroom. She stopped abruptly when she saw the enormous bed draped with a kingfisher blue duvet.

"What about…I mean you must have a spare room. You have haven't you?" she asked hopefully.

"Yes but that's what I'm trying to tell you. Someone's dismantled the bed and filled every available space with boxes. I didn't think to check earlier. I was too busy sorting out the problems that appeared out of nowhere and made their way to my desk while we were getting married."

She stared at the huge bed in despair, trying not to see the pictures it conjured up, pushing the memories of the past far back into the hidden recesses of her mind while she grappled with the immediate problem. Perhaps the spare room could be cleared; after all she hadn't brought much with her. Most of it was still in the house until she decided whether to sell or rent it out. She turned to the door opposite and pulled it open while Pierce watched her.

It was as impossible as he'd said. It was stacked to the ceiling with boxes, some of them hers and some of them obviously Pierce's put there for safe keeping until he moved into the house he was having built. Kerry hadn't seen it yet but she knew it was almost finished and that their stay in his suite of rooms at Greenleas would be a short one. The thought was no comfort now, however.

"Convinced?" He closed the door with a grim smile when she nodded. "Well what's it going to be then; half the bed and take your chances, or the couch?"

"The couch," she didn't hesitate but she wouldn't meet his eyes when she answered him because she didn't want him to see how much she wanted to share a bed with him again.

He sighed. "Okay you win, but don't expect to sleep well because it's as lumpy as hell."

She shrugged; glad to have won so easily. "I'll manage and I'll sort out the spare room in the morning."

And she had managed...just. She had tossed and turned for most of the night as she tried to get comfortable on the slippery leather cushions while most of her duvet slithered to the floor leaving her feet and legs bare. Miserably she had consoled herself with her meager triumph while experiencing a curious mixture of anger and relief. Anger that Pierce could joke about her sharing his bed and relief that she had managed to deny him despite herself.

On that thought she had finally fallen asleep and drifted into an erotic dream where her barely admitted subconscious wishes became an insubstantial reality as Pierce lifted her up and held her against his bare chest before sinking down with her into a tantalizing softness where arms and legs intertwined and his skin was warm and musky beneath her sleeping cheek.

* * *

She woke up with a start, disturbed by Lauren's voice calling her, and felt for her watch. It wasn't there, nor was the small coffee table where she'd placed it. She rolled over, clinging to the duvet so it wouldn't slip off again, and discovered she was alone in acres of kingfisher blue bed but that the pillow next to hers showed very definite signs of recent use.

She clutched at the buttons on the front of her pajamas with a harsh indrawn breath as the bedroom door burst open and Ben and Lauren hurtled into the room followed by a widely yawning Pierce who was still tying the sash of his dressing gown.

"They were calling for you," he said by way of an explanation, pushing his fingers through his hair until it stood up on end. Then he sat down on the edge of the bed as if there was nothing unusual about the situation.

She eyed him with alarm as fragments of her dream began to return in vivid detail. What had happened? At what point had her tightly repressed feelings broken free for long enough for her to end up in Pierce's bed. She must have started sleep walking again. It was something that had happened often when she was young and it still happened very occasionally now, especially when she was stressed. The demands of the past few days must have triggered it and if she wanted to avoid something like this happening again then she would have to start locking her bedroom door.

Chapter Eight

Ben brought her back to the here and now by discovering the acrobatic possibilities offered by such a vast area of pocket springing. His crow of triumph encouraged Lauren to clamber up beside him and the whole bed began to shake as they jumped in unison, effectively distracting Kerry from her attempt to remember exactly what had happened during the night as she tried to restrain them. Pierce chuckled as he caught the nearest wriggling body.

"That's how you wreck beds," he told an indignant and red-faced Ben. "I've got something much better that you can jump on after breakfast if you're very good."

"Bed?" Ben's initial protest was tempered by curiosity.

"No, not a bed. An enormous bouncy mat especially for little boys and girls."

"Ben bouncy now!" He pushed his legs sturdily against Pierce's thigh and stood up, balancing himself by grabbing a handful of hair.

"After breakfast," Pierce told him as he reached up and pried his son's fingers open with a rueful expression. The movement parted the front of his dressing gown so the silk fell aside and revealed a large expanse of muscled chest. Kerry looked away hurriedly, trying not to dwell on the fact that his legs were also bare. Instead she concentrated on Lauren who had collapsed into giggles across her lap.

"Is it like this every morning?" Pierce groaned, pulling Ben firmly onto his knee.

"Always. And it doesn't stop until bedtime." Kerry buried her face in Lauren's soft curls so she wouldn't have to look at him.

"Sounds like a good reason for hiring a nanny."

She jerked her head up and stared at him. "What happened to the full-time mother you were talking about three days ago?"

"I've decided I'd like her to be a part-time wife as well," the tone of Pierce's voice changed and a familiar huskiness sent a shiver of anticipation down Kerry's spine.

"You know that isn't part of the deal," she gathered Lauren closer and kissed the top of her head.

"Nor is sleeping in my bed." Despite the thickness of the duvet between them, his hand on her foot sent an instant flush of arousal through her body. When she finally looked at him her cheeks were hot and pink.

"I...don't understand...how it happened," she stuttered, the pink deepening to crimson when she saw the expression in his eyes. "I don't expect you to believe me but I thought I was dreaming."

He grinned at her. "You were. I heard you call out and thought you might be having trouble with Ben or Lauren but when I looked in on them everything was peaceful. You, however, were another matter entirely. You were thrashing around in some kind of nightmare with your duvet on the floor and you in imminent danger of following it."

"I don't remember any of it," Kerry tried to move her foot away from the heavy weight of his hand. He chuckled and gripped it tighter.

"I gave up wrestling with your covers when you threw your arms around my neck and kissed me. After that it seemed much more sensible to carry you in here rather than grapple about in the confines of a slippery couch, and you didn't exactly try to dissuade me."

Kerry's cheeks were on fire now she knew that parts of her dream were reality. How was she going to be able to explain away her behavior? Did he really believe her behavior was linked to sleepwalking or did he think she was just making excuses and that she really wanted to sleep with him after all? To cover her embarrassment she leapt to her own defense.

"If you knew I was dreaming, why didn't you wake me up?"

His grin widened. "And risk having my head bitten off? Besides sleeping with my wife seemed a pretty good idea to me, especially on our wedding night."

"But...but it wasn't like that," her confusion returned in force as she struggled to remember exactly what had happened during the night.

"Wasn't like what?" She could tell from the twinkle in his eyes that Pierce was enjoying her dilemma.

"Like...like...oh you know perfectly well what I mean," anger suddenly took over. "We might have spent some of the night together but we didn't make love."

"Didn't we?"

"You know we didn't," Kerry's voice was a wail of frustration. Ben stopped playing with his father's dressing gown cord and looked at her with interest.

"Mummy cross," he announced, his blue eyes twin replicas of Pierce's.

"No, she's just confused," Pierce lifted his hand and rumpled Ben's hair. The action released Kerry's foot.

She curled her legs away from him instantly and scowled when he laughed. He had no right to tease her like this. Last night had involved nothing more than the intimacy of sleeping in the same bed, which considering Pierce's apparent nakedness under his silk robe was bad enough. It wasn't fair of him to pretend there was more though.

"I am not confused. I remember exactly what happened."

"You must have been awake then," Pierce gave her a triumphant grin as she fell neatly into his trap. He stood up and hoisted Ben onto his shoulder without making any attempt to tidy the revealing front of his robe. Then he held out his hand to Lauren without giving Kerry a chance to reply.

"Come and help make Mummy a cup of coffee sweetheart."

She pulled her thumb out of her mouth and gave him a wide smile. "Mummy tired."

He leaned down, revealing more of his chest as he scooped her up into his arms. "You could say that. Mummy didn't sleep very well last night so let's give her a bit of peace and quiet shall we?"

He walked to the door with both children clinging, giggling, to his shoulders, leaving Kerry shaken by the effect of his body brushing against her as he plucked Lauren from her lap. Her arm tingled where he'd touched her and she could still smell his warm masculinity, a scent that was evocative of so many other nights when she'd shared his bed.

He paused and looked back at her, his face suddenly so serious she knew he was affected too. "Making love doesn't always end in sex Kerry. Nor does sex always involve making love. Those are the things you ought to think about while you sort out what actually happened between us last night."

* * *

Alone in the king sized bed, Kerry felt very vulnerable as his parting words washed over her. Was he trying to tell her he loved her after all? Had last night broken down the barriers between them and presented them with a chance of happiness. She closed her eyes against the brightness of the overhead light and let her tactile memory take over. She could recall the warmth of Pierce's arms about her and the tenderness of his mouth as it roamed across her face and neck and then further as his hands pushed the edges of her pajamas impatiently aside. She could remember her own reactions too. The erotic movements of her hands on his bare skin, her mouth clinging to his with something close to desperation, her body alive in a way it hadn't been for almost three years. He was right. They hadn't had sex but they had made love in those long moments before he'd wrapped her tightly in his arms and cradled her back into a deep sleep, soothing her with murmured words until she drifted away from that tearing need.

She opened her eyes wide. Why had he done it? Why had he forced his body into submission when it had pulsed with the same desperate desire as hers? She could still hear the groan of his frustration when he finally pulled her head onto his chest and made her go to sleep. Was it because he knew she wasn't properly awake or were there deeper reasons? She sat up and plumped the pillows behind her head. Whatever the reason, they had to talk about it because she couldn't live like this. She had to know how he really felt about her, had to know whether he was just playing with her or whether there was any sort of chance of rekindling the love they had once shared.

* * *

Lauren pushed the door open. "Pierce goin' out," she announced as Ben and Pierce followed her into the bedroom with identical frowns on their faces.

"Want bouncy," Ben's bottom lip was sticking out to an alarming degree as he glared at his father. "You said bouncy!"

"I know what I said," Pierce's frown deepened as he met Kerry's questioning gaze. "But that phone call said I must go out Ben. Someone is waiting to see me, someone I have to talk to. I'll take you to the gym and show you the bouncy mat when I come back."

He spoke to Ben but his explanation was as much for Kerry's benefit as he handed her a mug of coffee. Their fingers brushed as she took it from him and a pulse of instant attraction fired through her again.

His eyes darkened as he noted the way she moistened her lips with the tip of her tongue. "I'll try not to be long but there are one or two problems I must sort out, and quickly. It's one of the hazards of living on the premises I'm afraid. Everyone always assumes I'm instantly available."

She gave him a half smile, still shaken by the way her thoughts had been leading her before he returned to the bedroom. "We'll be fine won't we children? It'll give us a chance to get used to the apartment and find out where everything is."

He bent and kissed her, stopping the forced brightness of her reply as well as the beating of her heart as his mouth took possession of hers. The kiss only lasted a few seconds and her response was hampered by the mug of coffee in her hand and the fact that both children were watching with interest, but as he drew away she knew she no longer had any choice. Despite her inner struggle and her fierce protestations to the contrary, she was prepared to take him on almost any terms.

He saw the capitulation in her eyes and gently touched her cheek. "Don't go away."

She gave a shaky laugh. "Ben will see to that. He'll nag me to death until you come back and show him the bouncy mat."

He laughed as he moved away from the bed. "Tenacity is good but if you get desperate take them both along to the gym. I'll ask someone to put the landing mats into one of the anterooms for you. There's always a lull around nine-thirty, between the eager beavers and the Sunday morning regulars, so you'll probably have the place to yourselves."

He went into the adjoining bathroom as he spoke and before long she heard the splash of the shower. When he reappeared his hair was wet and water was trickling down the length of his bare back and soaking into the towel he'd wrapped round his waist. He chuckled at her expression as he opened a drawer and pulled out some fresh briefs.

"Close your eyes if it offends you so much."

She blushed into her mug of coffee and tried to ignore him. It wasn't easy and in the end she turned to the children in desperation and sent them to find a storybook so she could read to them.

"Why didn't I think of that?" Pierce had pulled on a pair of jeans and combed his hair into some semblance of order, but his shirt still dangled from his fingers. He tossed it onto the bed, moved swiftly across the room and took her in his arms. And this time, with her empty coffee mug on the bedside table and the twins out of the way, there was nothing to hamper Kerry except her own doubts; doubts that faded into insignificance when his lips claimed hers because this time there was nothing tentative about his kiss. It had all the desperation of a drowning man and she felt his urgency in her own response as she locked her arms around his neck until the smooth surface of his still damp chest rested against her breast. With a tortured groan his hands began to explore the hidden curves of her body, his fingers tangling with the cotton of her pajamas while his lips continued to devour her until the children's reappearance drove them apart.

He stood up, thrust his arms into his shirt and then failed to fasten the buttons because his fingers were shaking too much. He gave her a rueful smile. "There appear to be more disadvantages than advantages to fatherhood so far."

She shrugged, not bothering to hide her amusement. "You'll get used to it."

"If that's meant to make me feel better, it doesn't," he slipped his feet into his shoes and headed for the door.

"Kiss!" Ben bounced up from the bed indignantly.

"I just did fella. What are you doing, keeping tabs?" Pierce paused in the doorway and laughed.

"Kiss Ben!"

"Hey what's this, a takeover bid?" Pierce returned to the bed and dropped a kiss on his son's upturned face, following it up with a kiss for Lauren. Kerry smiled at him, her mouth still rosy and moist.

"You seem to have scored a hit."

"With all the family?" His lips were close to hers as he waited for her answer.

When she nodded he kissed her hard, leaving a promise imprinted on her lips so that when she started reading to the children her voice was breathless and the words jumped and blurred across the page.

* * *

By nine thirty Kerry's patience was near breaking point. Although she'd read countless stories to the children, dressed them, raided

159

Pierce's fridge for eggs because he didn't appear to have any cereal or fruit juice, and showered and dressed herself, he still hadn't returned. She poured a second mug of coffee hoping the caffeine would help her to concentrate on the children's chatter. She wished she could find something to take her mind of the immediate future, but after shaking the duvet into shape and tidying the children's beds, there was nothing else to do. She'd washed up, sorted through their clothes and loaded the washing machine. All that was left was the anticipation of Pierce's return and it was preventing her from settling. At any other time she would have played happily with Ben and Lauren or, given their immersion in a game of their own, would have taken grateful advantage of a few moments of peace. Instead she found herself wishing she'd been able to persuade Mel to move Melanie's Kitchen to Greenleas straight away instead of waiting until the end of the following week. That, at least, would have kept her busy.

"Bounce!" Ben's reminder broke into her thoughts and she seized on it with relief. Pierce had said he would get the mats laid out in one of the anterooms in the gym and as she already knew where the gym was she would take him and Lauren herself. Anything was better than sitting and waiting.

She held out her hands to the twins. "Come on. Let's go and find that bouncy mat."

"Pierce?" Lauren questioned hopefully as she took Kerry's outstretched hand.

Kerry shook her head. "No. Pierce won't be there, just the bouncy mat."

She opened the door that led directly into the sports complex with a slight frown as she reviewed what she had just said. Should she start referring to Pierce as Daddy, or was it something that would just happen once they were used to living with him. He hadn't said anything about it so perhaps he didn't mind. She made a mental note to discuss it with him as she stepped out into the corridor and turned in the direction of the gym.

Although several people eyed her curiously as she walked past them holding Ben and Lauren firmly by their hands, she didn't notice because she was too intent on the new direction her thoughts were taking her. Now the barriers seemed to be coming down between Pierce and herself there were so many questions to be answered, so many decisions to be made before they could begin to make a real life for themselves and the children.

She sighed as she turned the corner. And even if things were better between them, would it be enough? Could he ever truly forgive her for hiding his children from him? She doubted it. And how long would it be before he began to find parenthood irksome?

Ben, sensing an opportunity, took advantage of her absentmindedness, wriggled his hand free and started to run. His actions brought her back to the present in double quick time. Ben out of control and running as fast as he could through Greenleas Country Club was a nightmare she didn't want to experience. Holding onto Lauren more tightly she lengthened her stride. She was a moment too late though and he grabbed the handle of the first door he came to before she could stop him. It swung open soundlessly as she drew level and she only managed to prevent him from darting inside by grabbing the seat of his pants.

Hoisting him onto one hip she opened her mouth to apologies to the people in the room. Pierce and Marissa hadn't noticed anything amiss, however, because they were far too busy kissing one another.

For a long moment Kerry was too stunned to move as the sight of Pierce perched on the edge of the desk while Marissa pressed herself against him, her long red fingernails like splashes of blood in his tangle of hair, rendered her speechless. Then a blind, unreasoning anger took over, sweeping her away from the doorway and back to the apartment despite Ben's protests.

"We'll find the bouncy mat later," she told him. "Right now there are a few things Mummy has to do."

* * *

When Pierce eventually returned, shortly before lunch, he found it difficult to get into the apartment. Squeezing past a stack of cardboard boxes he stood in the doorway of the spare room and surveyed the prevailing chaos with amusement.

"Are we expecting visitors?"

Kerry looked up from her third attempt at reassembling the bed with a fierce scowl. "I would be able to fit this damned bed together more easily if I took up weight training!"

He stepped over the boxes cluttering the doorway and lifted the bed's heavy wooden base without any apparent effort. She slotted the legs into position and then waited until he lowered it to the floor before attempting to heave the mattress onto the bed.

He chuckled as he helped her and then pushed the whole thing back against the wall. "I see what you mean about needing something to do but in future it might be better to choose something less physical. There was no urgency about sorting this room anyway. I was quite happy for it to stay as it was until the house is ready."

"Well I wasn't!" Kerry shrugged off the arm he placed across her shoulders and picked up a pile of bedding. "I have no intention of going through last night's fiasco again, nor do I intend to spend the next few weeks sleeping on the couch, so if you'll just move out the way I'll make the bed up. I want to get as much of my stuff unpacked as possible before the twins wake up from their morning nap."

"What the hell are you talking about Kerry? You seemed happy enough in my bed this morning." He caught at her arm as she pushed past him and swung her round to face him.

"That was this morning," she wrenched herself away from him angrily and began to make up the bed with swift, furious movement. "I've had plenty of time to think since then thanks to your problem visitor. Did you get everything sorted out to your mutual satisfaction by the way?"

He groaned as he leaned against the wall. "You saw Marissa didn't you? I knew someone had walked in on us but I never imagined it was you."

"I'm surprised you noticed anything at all given how occupied you were; and it was Ben who walked in on you, just in case he starts asking awkward questions."

She finished fitting the bottom sheet and reached for the pillow but Pierce was too quick for her. He seized it and held it just out of reach as he waited for her to come closer. She gave him a withering look.

"I'm not in the mood for those kinds of games Pierce. Save them for Marissa. In fact save everything for Marissa because I'm not about to take out shares in you. I'm an all or nothing kind of person, so as far as our relationship is concerned you can go to hell."

Pierce pushed himself away from the wall and walked towards her, tossing the pillow carelessly onto the bed. "And I can take Marissa with me I suppose. Doesn't it ever occur to you that things might not be what they seem? You made the same mistake when you ran out on me. Because you heard me say I didn't want children you took away my right to fatherhood without giving me a choice. Now you're doing the same with Marissa. You're acting as judge, jury and executioner without giving me a chance to explain."

She stood her ground defiantly, not even wincing when he gripped her tightly by the shoulders. "From what I saw this morning there is only one thing that needs explaining which is why you bothered to marry me in the first place. With your money and contacts you could probably have the children living with you in a matter of weeks."

"Could but haven't," his grip tightened. "What do you think I am Kerry, a self-serving masochist? If that's what you thought this morning was about then there's no hope for us. What else do I have to do to convince you that I want you as well as the children? In the bedroom this morning I thought we were getting somewhere but obviously I was wrong. Do you always view the world from where you're standing because if you do then it's time you climbed down from your high horse and joined the rest of us a ground level."

"Finding you again, and then marrying you so quickly, has thrown my life into as much disarray as yours you know, so it's hardly surprising I forgot all about a longstanding lunch date with Marissa. When you walked in on us today I was trying to convince her she had no future with me without actually telling her why. If she'd learned about you and the children she would have gone straight to the media out of spite."

"I'm sure she found your methods of persuasion very convincing. I know I did."

He shook her in a fury of frustration. "You haven't the faintest notion about anything. You're still a child Kerry, despite the struggle you've had over the past three years, and like a child you can't see further than the nose on your face. If you'd stayed longer, interrupted us even, you'd have learned the truth."

She glared up at him, her shoulders hunched against his anger. "Don't take me for a complete fool Pierce. Maggie told me all about you and Marissa and about how everyone expected her to be Mrs Pierce Simon before long."

"Well if you already know so much then you should be able to find a bit of compassion for her. Marissa has feelings too Kerry, something you seem to have overlooked in your general paranoia. What sort of person would I be if I shook her briefly by the hand and showed her the door like an unwanted salesman?"

Kerry was only too aware of Marissa's feelings. She had been at the receiving end of them too often in the past to appreciate Pierce's concern. Marissa was bitchy and narcissistic and she had never been nice to Kerry. The memory of all the put downs she had experienced at the other girl's hands added to the jealousy and hurt that had been eating at her all morning, and produced an explosion of reaction. Angrily she pulled herself free.

"I don't care what sort of person you think you are when I know the truth. As far as I'm concerned you can do exactly as you like from now on. You can even take Marissa out for the lunch which you so kindly cancelled on my behalf."

He stared at her for a moment, his face tight with anger, and then he turned on his heel and made for the door, kicking boxes out of his way in a fury of movement.

"Thanks for the suggestion. I'll do just that!" And he was gone; slamming the door behind him while Kerry sank down onto the bed and stared blindly into space.

Chapter Nine

Pierce didn't return until just before the twin's teatime. They were drawing at the kitchen table while Kerry attempted to make the spare room habitable by pushing as many boxes as possible under the bed. He ignored her as he walked through to the kitchen, only to reappear moments later with Ben and Lauren in tow.

"We're going to the gym," he told her unsmilingly. "Do you want to come too?"

She shook her head, not trusting herself to speak. Lauren, already out of sorts due to Kerry's short temper during the day, dragged on her hand with a plaintive whine.

"Mummy come," she demanded, loath to leave behind a mother who was being so uncharacteristically inconsistent in case she changed again while she and Ben were with Pierce. Recognizing the signs of insecurity Kerry gave in and followed the three of them into the corridor.

Greenleas was much busier now and there were a lot of people wandering about in designer jogging kits and expensive sports shoes. She sighed. Pierce's life hadn't changed; it had merely altered its direction. He was still part of the glamour of a sport that rewarded its best players handsomely, and he was still surrounding himself with wealthy people whatever he said about remembering the less affluent days of his childhood.

She wondered if things would change once the whole complex was complete and it was opened up to a wider mix of people. Pierce had told her and Mel about his plans for the future; how he wanted to develop a tennis-training centre that would link with schools, and how he was going to do the same with golf eventually too. Perhaps the rarified atmosphere would fade once it stopped being an exclusive membership club.

"Come 'long," Lauren pulled at her hand impatiently as she sensed her mother's mind wandering.

With a tired smile, Kerry obeyed. She listened to Lauren's chatter as they followed Ben and Pierce down the long corridor leading to the gym but it didn't distract her enough to stop her noticing how alike they were. Ben's shoulders were just as square and although he was barely two, he moved in the same way, using an economy of effort and, despite the slightly rolling gait of his chubby legs, with a noticeable athleticism. She gritted her teeth and looked away. It was bad enough having to live with Pierce let alone be reminded of him every time she looked at his son.

When they reached the gym she followed reluctantly, pulled along by an excited Lauren who trotted past the complicated array of shiny equipment without a second glance so intent was she on catching up with Pierce and Ben before they found the bouncy mat. Pierce glanced behind him and laughed when he saw her eagerness.

"Don't use all your energy up before you get there, angel. The mat won't go away."

* * *

The small anteroom was stacked with extra equipment including rolled up netting, a ball machine full of used tennis balls and a couple of exercise bikes. Pierce pointed towards a pile of enormously thick landing mats that were spread across the floor. They were bright blue and looked well used. Ben ran across the floor and attempted to climb up on his own but Lauren hung back in sudden trepidation.

Pierce gave his son a boost and then held onto him for long enough to explain why he needed to stay well away from the edge. "If you don't," he said, "you'll fall off and hurt yourself, and then you won't be able to bounce anymore."

Ben listened solemnly. He liked the blue mats. They felt squashy and wobbly under his feet and he wanted to jump all over them, but he wasn't going to if Pierce told him not to because he didn't like it when Pierce got cross with him.

Kerry, watching, could almost read his thoughts. She gave an inward sigh. If only she could have the same sort of authority over him then Pierce would be superfluous, but unfortunately that wasn't going to happen. Even at two Ben had a mind of his own and in recent months she'd found herself struggling with him as he started to exert his will. In her worst moments she had even begun to wonder how she would cope with him when he was older. Now she knew. It was Pierce who would cope with him. He would be the one who was prepared to say no and who would set the sort of rules necessary to keep an impulsive child, like Ben, safe. She just wished she could feel more grateful.

She looked down to where Lauren was still clutching her hand. She, at least, was less of a problem. As long as Kerry was somewhere around Lauren was content.

"Do you want to climb up too or shall I lift you?" Pierce bent down until his face was level with his daughter's and gave her an encouraging smile. She pushed her thumb into her mouth and shook her head.

"You don't need to be frightened sweetheart. It's really easy once you're up there. Look at Ben. See what fun he's having. Come on, I'll climb up with you and hold your hand if you like."

Very slowly Lauren wriggled her fingers out of Kerry's hand and transferred them to Pierce. He smiled at her as he led her across to the mats and lifted her onto them. Then, with a casual hitch of his hips, he joined her, and before long both children were squealing with delight as he bounced and jumped with them. When he was sure Lauren was confident enough for him to leave her, he retreated to the edge of the mats with a grin.

"They should sleep well after this."

His tone, as he glanced at Kerry, was polite but cool, and she recognized it. It was the voice he used with people who didn't hold his interest but who warranted common courtesy. It cut her to the quick although she knew better than to expect anything else. After all she had blown his cover as far as Marissa was concerned, spoiling any hope he might have cherished of keeping them both happy. No! A distant politeness was all she could expect now and she would have to be satisfied with that while she searched for a way to get on with her own life.

* * *

She was rapidly proved right. From the moment they argued over Marissa, Pierce ceased to be interested in her. He rarely sought her out, only spoke when he needed to, and never tried to pursue the intimacy of their first night together. At the same time, however, he remained courteous and thoughtful, bringing her an early morning mug of coffee with all the impersonality of a waiter, and making sure he took the children off her hands at least once during the day. Now that their relationship was devoid of any sort of emotional conflict their life together quickly settled into a routine.

Not that Kerry had much time to brood because by the end of the following week she and Mel were too busy planning the future of Melanie's Kitchen for her to give much thought to anything else. They dreamt up and discarded a number of unlikely plans before submitting their final suggestions to Pierce for his approval. He was cautiously enthusiastic.

"Don't try to do too much at first," he warned. "I like your ideas but I think you need to curb your enthusiasm. Start small and expand. Continual development is always better than having to cut back. How about offering a limited lunch menu alongside the usual coffee, juice and donuts, and then moving into breakfasts for the early morning regulars once your reputation starts growing. Light suppers could come later."

Mel shook her head decisively. "Not good enough when part of the deal is to promote Greenleas. If the main restaurant and the conference centre are going to provide the sort of high quality meals you say they are, then we need to as well, although faster and at a fraction of the price. Melanie's Kitchen is for people who are in a rush...you know, the executive visiting the conference centre who likes to swim before breakfast, or go to the gym, instead of spending forty minutes eating a cooked breakfast in the restaurant. And then there are the young mums who will come in after dropping their kids off at school. Lots of them won't have had time for breakfast or, if they have, it will have been a rushed affair. They'll appreciate a leisurely coffee or maybe juice and toast. They might like to meet friends for a light lunch as well… as long as we can keep our prices down."

He eyed her thoughtfully. "You're right of course, but can you manage it?"

"Yes…with the right support."

"Which is?"

"Our own kitchen and a small office where we can plan our menus and cope with all the paperwork."

"No extra investment or special favors?"

"None. We're an independent company and all we ask is the chance to reorganize things, and manage your outdated bistro our way."

She didn't tell him Kerry had already put her house in the hands of an agent and that the money she would raise was what was going to hold them together for the first few months. She didn't understand Kerry's need for secrecy but she wasn't going to give her away.

She had given up trying to reconcile this new unsmiling Kerry with the laughing girl she had known before Pierce came onto the scene. It wasn't her business unless her friend decided to share it with her, but Melanie's Kitchen was, so if Kerry was prepared to sink her money into the company then she wasn't going to complain.

Kerry gave an apologetic smile when Mel glanced at her. She knew the secret about her

174

money was safe but she wished she could tell her friend the truth. It would be a relief to talk to her about everything but she wasn't going to do it because it wouldn't be fair to any of them. If she and Mel and Pierce were all going to be working together then the least she could do was to keep emotion out of it and make sure everything stayed on a professional footing. Besides, she wasn't sure she could explain the situation to Mel any more, not when she was still puzzling over it herself.

She was still no clearer as to why Pierce had insisted on marrying her when it would have been so easy for him to say she was an unfit parent and fight for custody. She guessed she would have to believe him when he said it was for the children because he was proving to be a very good father. He mixed fun with discipline and affection while maintaining a healthy disregard for the small bumps and falls sustained when they were playing. Already they were responding to him more and more. They were less inclined to whine and cry when they fell over too. And most of all they no longer worried if Kerry wasn't with them.

She watched him as he bent over Mel's meticulously detailed lists and wished things could have been different. For the briefest moment she even wished she hadn't walked in on him and Marissa. If she hadn't known about their relationship then perhaps things would have worked out, but knowing had unbalanced the equation, so now it was impossible for her to behave in any other way. With the memory of Marissa between them everything they did was shadowed by separateness, even the time they shared with the children.

As if he sensed her thoughts, Pierce suddenly raised his head and looked straight at her. His eyes were very blue as they reflected the winter sunlight streaming in through the window. "What's your view of all this Kerry?" It was the first time he'd spoken to her directly that day.

She gave him a frosty smile. "I agree with Mel. It's an all or nothing situation. Any attempt to mix catering standards will affect your reputation. You need everyone who visits Greenleas to rave about it when they meet their friends."

His answering smile was edged with a scornful amusement that didn't quite reach his eyes. "And that's from an expert on how all or nothing situations affect my reputation as I remember it."

Kerry paled slightly as he referred to the words she had spat at him when she found out about Marissa, but she kept her head high as he turned back to Mel.

"Okay. Go ahead and plan for excellence! The bistro is yours as from the beginning of next month. My only stipulation is that Ben and Lauren aren't neglected so maybe you'd better talk my wife into employing a qualified nanny because until then she isn't available."

Kerry bit her lip as she wondered why he was suddenly pushing for all out war. It wasn't like him to involve other people, least of all Mel who he appeared to like and respect. She glanced at her friend apologetically.

"Actually I have an idea of my own about that. I think we should open up a daycare and employ qualified nursery nurses to run it. If we do that then Ben and Lauren will meet other children and be able to play safely when we're both busy. It will also make it easier for young mums with babies and very small children to use the sports facilities during the day. You could even offer them a special price for the times when the gym and pool are under-utilized."

Mel and Pierce both stared at her. She gave a short, bitter laugh. "Don't look so flabbergasted. I do have the occasional idea of my own you know."

Mel shook her head admiringly. "I think it's a terrific suggestion. And much better than employing a nanny who would be around all the time, even when you don't need her."

Kerry nodded. "The children are already showing signs of missing their nursery school but it's too far away from Greenleas to make taking them there practical. A journey across town can take anything up to half-an-hour, which makes it too long a morning for them, whereas a daycare, here, would keep them occupied without the additional strain of a long car journey.

She looked at Pierce and surprised a faint hint of admiration in his eyes instead of the frown she was expecting. He smiled. "Sounds good to me. I've been trying to think of a way to attract more mid-week sportsmen and women and this sounds like the answer. How long do you need to plan it?"

Kerry found herself smiling back at him. "Hardly any time at all if you'll give me the space I need and the necessary funding. I've already talked to the owner of the nursery the twins used to attend and she's keen to have a go. She's been talking about expanding for ages so the thought of starting a daycare here had her practically drooling. Mary has signed up as a helper too."

Mel gave a peal of laughter. "Trust Mum! She's never said a word to me about either. Do you always play your cards so close to your chest Kerry?"

"Always," Pierce answered for her, but this time he was laughing and he rested his hand briefly on Kerry's shoulder as they walked Mel back to reception.

* * *

After that, things changed...not least Pierce's attitude towards Kerry. He was still reserved but the coolness had gone and he spoke to her often, discussing his plans for Greenleas and even occasionally asking for her opinion, or, in the case of catering, her advice. It was the start of a new relationship between them where the traumas of the past were patched over with a new respect as well as a realization that they both had something to offer as they attempted to build a new life together.

Kerry continued to sleep in the spare room and Pierce made no attempt to dissuade her, but when he delivered her early morning mug of coffee he now sometimes stayed to talk to her, telling her what he was doing that day or listening to her own plans with every sign of interest. It had an effect on the twins as well. Soon Ben became far more manageable and Lauren stopped whining when she couldn't have her own way.

As the weeks went by Kerry became more hopeful they had at last found a way to leave all their squabbles behind them. She was aware she still had one problem to overcome, however. Marissa!

From newspaper articles she knew she was filming an American game show to be shown in the New Year. She also knew she would soon be back in England for a promotional guest appearance on a late night chat show and it was that that she was dreading. Once Marissa was back in the country things between Kerry and Pierce would change. His girlfriend's return would inevitably stretch his newfound delight in his family to the utmost.

She was lying awake early one morning thinking about this, and about the fact he hadn't yet mentioned visiting his parents even though he'd now telephoned them with the news of his marriage, when she suddenly realized it was his birthday. She counted back to their wedding day; amazed so much time had flown by without her noticing. It was now November and today was Pierce's thirty-fourth birthday.

She lay still for a few moments longer and then, hearing the children chattering in the next room, pushed back her covers and tiptoed into their bedroom. Ben and Lauren looked at her in surprise because they had only been awake for a few minutes and they were used to being the first ones astir. She laughed at their solemn, wide-eyed expressions.

"Come along you two. We're going shopping."

"Breakfast?" Ben suggested hopefully, not entirely concurring with her suggestion.

"You can have breakfast later. Right now we have to go and buy Pierce a birthday card."

They didn't really understand but Kerry's enthusiasm was enough to convince them something exciting was going to happen, so they popped out from beneath their matching duvets with wide smiles and let her dress them with more cooperation than usual. She kissed them both and then led them through to her bedroom.

"Be very quiet now because Pierce is asleep," she told them as she hastily pulled on a pair of jeans and a thick sweater.

* * *

It was almost eight o'clock when they arrived back at Greenleas having plundered the only shop open at that hour in the morning, the local newsagent. Ben and Lauren were each clutching birthday cards and small white paper bags, while Kerry's purchase was wrapped in brown paper. She was also carrying a box of chocolate beans and several cake decorations.

They crept in through the side door with exaggerated whisperings and tiptoed down the passageway to Pierce's bedroom. The children were pink cheeked with excitement.

"Pierce sleep?" Lauren demanded.

Kerry pushed open the bedroom door the tiniest crack. "I don't know darling. Why don't you go and find out."

Lauren looked alarmed at this suggestion but Ben needed no further encouragement. He flung the door wide with great élan and dived into the room, landing on the bed without bothering to check if Pierce was awake. Lauren remained slightly more circumspect, clinging hold of Kerry's hand and trying to pull her into the room after her.

Gently Kerry disengaged her fingers and gave her daughter a little push, not wishing to intrude too much on something that belonged to Pierce. She was also uncomfortably aware that he was awake and sitting on the side of his bed clad, as far as she could tell, in nothing more than a towel.

He looked up, startled, as Ben burst through the doorway and the eyes that met Kerry's were like thunderclouds; a dark stormy grey without a trace of blue. She gave an involuntary shiver when she saw the outward manifestation of the anger that she knew must always be burning inside him, an anger that could only be directed at her. She sensed something else too, in the brief moment before the children's excitement shattered the tension. It was a dark despair that stabbed at her like an emotional knife, destroying what little peace of mind she had managed to achieve over the past few weeks.

Was this how he really felt about her? Was she responsible for this peculiar reduction in his personality? She closed her eyes against a truth she didn't want to face. How he must hate her for having destroyed so much; the plans he had made with Marissa, the chance of a normal family life, and the loss of his children's early years. She couldn't bear it, couldn't bear to be the cause of so much suffering. There must be another way they could live.

* * *

"Aren't you going to join us?" Pierce's voice broke through the barrier of her misery. It was full of all the old enticements; soft, slightly husky, questioning. She opened her eyes and found she was being scrutinized by three pairs of identical blue eyes, all of them smiling and waiting for her to say something.

She stared at Pierce in bewilderment. With Ben and Lauren sitting one on either knee, he looked relaxed, the harsh grooves of unhappiness that had lined his cheeks erased by a wide smile that included her.

"We can't open my presents without you," he put out a hand and waited for her to take it.

Slowly she moved towards the bed. "Happy birthday," she had to clear her throat before she could speak. "I'm afraid we left it a bit late so you'll have to be content with what the newsagent had to offer."

He peered into the bag Ben thrust under his nose and grinned. "I have a passion for sugar mice, surely you know that."

"Me too! Me too!" Lauren bounced up and down on his knee impatiently while he looked in her bag. With a grin he extracted two jelly babies from the mass that had stuck together thanks to the heat of her small hands, and popped one into each of the children's mouths.

Kerry's earlier depression dissolved into laughter when she saw the bemused expression on his face. "Ben and Lauren chose their own presents," she explained.

He shook his head admiringly, hugging the children to him while his eyes danced with amusement above their heads. "I'd never have guessed. How did they know exactly what I like?"

"Ben like!" His son wriggled indignantly out of his father's arms, his mouth still full of jelly baby, and peered longingly into the bag containing the sugar mouse.

Pierce grinned as he lifted it out of reach. "Not until after breakfast young man, and I'm having the head."

"Ben stuck out his lip mutinously. "Me head!"

"Oh Ben, it's Pierce's present. He can eat it all if he wants to. Come on, show him his birthday card." In an attempt to distract Ben she picked up the envelope that he'd dropped on the floor.

It did the trick. Both children immediately tore the envelopes off their cards and held them up for inspection, pointing excitedly to where they'd each scrawled a smudged kiss in red crayon with Kerry's help. Pierce took both cards and admired them obediently, commenting on the pictures and the children's expertise with the crayon in equal proportion, but Kerry was aware of a change in his voice as he read the identical message on the front of each card.

"Thank you." His kisses were for the twins but Kerry knew the words were directed at her as he carefully displayed the cards on his bedside table so the words Happy Birthday Daddy were easy to read. She ignored the lump in her throat, telling herself he would shortly revert to the cool, distant individual she was used to. With an effort she held out her own present.

"It was the best I could do in the circumstances. I forgot it was your birthday until I woke up this morning."

He took it without a word, letting the twins wriggle out of his grasp as he did so, so she was suddenly alone with his near nakedness and uncomfortably aware of the length of his bare legs as they stretched out beside her. She started to get up, using the twin's breakfast as an excuse, but Pierce caught hold of her hand and pulled her back down.

"You can't go until I've opened my present can she children?" Ben and Lauren were now sitting on the floor at his feet peering hopefully into the envelopes they'd discarded. They grinned up at him as they shook their heads.

"It isn't much," she said as he began to unwrap it. "If I'd remembered yesterday I'd have gone into town and found something better."

She had bought him a book; thanking her lucky stars the newsagent was forward thinking enough to display a variety of possible gifts next to the birthday cards. It was the latest offering by one of his favorite authors and she hoped it was recent enough for him not to have read it yet.

He read the blurb on the cover and then turned towards her and hugged her, his hands warm through the soft wool of her sweater. "You remembered how much I like his books. Thank you."

She shrugged self-consciously; too aware of his physical presence to ignore the weight of his arm on her shoulders but glad he liked the book. She wished he'd stop looking at her like that.

Embarrassed by his scrutiny she forced a lighthearted laugh.

"I guess a special breakfast is in order too. Come on children, come and help me. And later on we'll make daddy a birthday cake."

"You mean I get to have cake as well," suddenly the old familiar Pierce was back in force as he released her and stood up, sweeping Lauren up from where she'd been playing by his feet and tossing her into the air.

She gave a giggle that was half terror, half excitement, and clutched at his hair. Immediately Ben clambered up onto the bed and held his arms wide, demanding equal rights. His father complied, leaving Kerry free to slip silently from the room to prepare breakfast, wishing as she did so she could wipe the memory of Pierce's muscular chest and arms right out of her mind.

* * *

The rest of the day passed without incident, with Mel, Mary and George arriving in the early afternoon to share Pierce's birthday cake for the children's benefit. Tea was a relaxed affair and after Ben and Lauren had each blown out the candles twice, the conversation quickly turned to Mary's involvement in the newly organized daycare. She talked about it enthusiastically for about ten minutes until she noticed the slightly glazed expression on Pierce's face and gave a self-conscious laugh.

"Sorry! I know I get a bit carried away."

George rolled his eyes as he gave a good natured chuckle. "That's a slight understatement love. You've been talking about it so much you've forgotten to offer our services for this evening yet."

"Goodness, I quite forgot. We thought you might like us to babysit for you so you can go out and celebrate Pierce's birthday together."

"Thank you…" Kerry began to refuse, wondering how she could do it tactfully, because the last thing she wanted was to upset Mary and George. She didn't want them to think their offer wasn't appreciated, but nor did she want to give them an insight into nature of the true relationship between herself and Pierce.

"…and yes please," Pierce finished the sentence for her with a smile of thanks. "It's a wonderful idea now Ben and Lauren are settled. Besides, Kerry could do with a night off before the conference centre and hotel open officially and Melanie's Kitchen gets into full swing."

"Mmm. I agree with you. She's been looking a bit peaky lately." Mel, who knew Kerry well enough to gauge all her moods, fixed her with an unrepentant gaze as she backed up the others. "We'll put the children to bed for you if you like and give you a chance to make a real night of it. You need some time out to enjoy yourselves."

Kerry frowned. Somehow Pierce and Mel had maneuvered her into a corner; Pierce because for some reason it suited him, and Mel because she thought she knew what was best for Kerry. They were both too bossy by half. Suddenly she thought of a way to turn the tables on them.

"I've just remembered…it's Mel's birthday on Monday, so she can come too and we can have a double celebration," she turned to Pierce with every appearance of surprise that such a happy coincidence should exist.

The glint in his eyes could have been relief or anger for all Kerry cared. It was enough that courtesy demanded he back up her invitation and that Mel, finding herself outnumbered by two to one, was forced to give in. With a sigh of relief she began to clear the table. At least she wouldn't have to spend an evening alone in a candlelit restaurant with Pierce. With Mel there, the conversation would remain impersonal and businesslike and she was going to keep it at that level until she'd had more time to think.

The expression on Pierce's face when she and the children had surprised him sitting alone in his bedroom that morning was still haunting her. Given long enough surely she would be able to come up with a solution that would leave him free to live his own life without it affecting his relationship with the children. Right now though she needed time and she was buying it with Mel's reluctant presence, and to hell with both of them.

Chapter Ten

The restaurant was dimly lit and Kerry felt a shiver of apprehension as Pierce waited for her to sit down. What she had considered a good idea earlier seemed far less attractive now she was face to face with him across the table. His apparent good humor was belied by the dark glint in his eyes every time he looked at her, and she wondered if he was going to pay her back for arranging the evening to suit her own needs. She jutted her chin defiantly. She was being ridiculous. After all what could he possibly do in a crowded restaurant with Mel in tow?

She soon found out when he stood up to greet a blond giant of a man of about his own age who was threading his way between the tables. "David! I'm so glad you could make it. You remember Kerry of course, and this is Mel, her friend and business partner."

David Merrick shook hands with Mel and then kissed Kerry on the cheek before he slid into the empty chair between them. "He finally tracked you down then Kerry. When Marissa finds out she'll start spitting blood."

"You'll note David hasn't lost any of his subtlety or tact," Pierce's voice was full of a grim humor as he spoke to Kerry. "Still as he lost a tennis partner when I left the circuit to look for you, I guess he's entitled."

She was saved from answering by the reappearance of their waiter. By the time they had all decided what they wanted to eat and Pierce had ordered wine, the direction of the conversation had changed and she breathed a sigh of relief as she listened to Mel telling David about Melanie's Kitchen.

He asked so many questions about it and about Greenleas that his interest took them right through the first course. Then Pierce began to talk about his plans to develop the sports complex even further, and as the others began to respond to his enthusiasm she started to relax and stop worrying. He didn't have an ulterior motive in inviting David back into their lives without any warning. She guessed he had just wanted someone to even up the numbers and David was available.

She remembered how the two men had always managed to stay friends despite the fact that tensions on court had sometimes overlapped into their personal relationship. And David had always been nice to her too, treating her as someone special to Pierce, not as if she was just a continuation of a stream of girls who were virtually interchangeable, and often too star-struck to make intelligent conversation.

Briefly she wondered what was behind Pierce's throwaway remark and then dismissed it as being ridiculous. Of course he hadn't abandoned his career to look for her. She forced herself to forget about him and concentrate on the others and was amused by Mel's vivacity. Maybe Pierce had unwittingly done her friend a favor by inviting David to join them because Mel was positively sparkling, and her conversation seemed to be concentrating all of David's attention too.

"They make a good pair don't they?" Pierce leaned towards her and touched her arm, jolting her thoughts into disarray as she suddenly realized what else he had achieved by inviting David. With the other two in full flow she was as alone with him as if Mel had never been invited. She swallowed nervously.

"They certainly seem to get along well together."

"Does that surprise you?" His fingers were still brushing her wrist just below the sleeve of the pink wool dress she had worn for their wedding.

"Not really. They're both such strong personalities and they have lots of different interests, so I suppose it was inevitable they'd find a lot to talk about."

He gave a satisfied smile. "That's what I thought when I called David to see if he was free."

She started worrying again. He grinned when he saw her expression.

"Of course I did have another reason for inviting him."

She shrugged, concentrating on her wine.

"Don't you want to know what it is, Kerry?" Suddenly his fingers locked over hers with such urgency she was forced to look at him. "I invited him so I could have a little time alone with my wife, something which is becoming increasingly difficult now we're so close to launching the sports complex."

"You see I think...hope... you're ready to hear what I intend to tell you tonight. I've been trying to find a way for days but every time we have a moment alone together you slip away from me or invite someone else to join us. So tonight I came up with the grand idea of occupying Mel with David, particularly as he's one of the few people who knows the whole story, which gives me the chance to redress the balance a little."

She stared at him. She didn't have the first clue what he was talking about but she was frightened by the expression in his eyes. In the dim lighting they seemed to be full of the same despair and anger she had glimpsed that morning. Surely he wasn't going to wash their dirty linen in such a public place. She glanced around, wondering if people at the nearby tables were aware of the strain between herself and Pierce, and wondering, too, why Mel and David seemed quite oblivious to the tension.

"Why here?" She kept her voice low, struggling for calm and hoping she could find a way to distract him.

His answering smile didn't hold any humor as he stared over her shoulder. "It was a question of bringing the mountain to Mohamed I'm afraid."

Puzzled, and sensing a black fury she couldn't understand, she turned her head to follow his gaze and saw he was looking at two people sitting at a table in the far corner of the restaurant. Whoever they were they had obviously only just arrived because a waiter was still fussing with their chairs. When he finally moved away she saw the woman was a tanned and exotic looking Marissa, whose stunning figure was poured into a scarlet sheath dress. Her face turned pale. At last she understood. He had brought her here to humiliate her. I would only be a matter of time before Marissa saw them and then Pierce would cross to her table with a cleverly contrived exclamation of surprise and invite her and her companion to join them. She had no doubt it was something they'd cooked up between them, a way of showing Kerry she wasn't going to interfere with their relationship, that life would go on in the same old way despite her.

* * *

The next twenty minutes seemed like an eternity as their waiter arrived with the main course and the flow of conversation became more general again. Pierce continued to behave normally with only an occasional glance into the far corner but Kerry was too shaken by his obvious interest to do more than make a token attempt at her meal. For a long time nobody commented on her silence but eventually Mel spoke to her.

"Are you feeling okay Kerry? You're awfully quiet."

She opened her mouth to reply, to say there was nothing to worry about but as she did so Marissa shifted slightly, her elegantly manicured hands gesturing in such a way that Kerry was momentarily distracted by the reflection she could see in the mirror tiles on the wall in front of her. Involuntarily she turned her head to see who she was talking to. At that exact moment Marissa's escort threw back his head and gave a throaty laugh. If Kerry had been pale before, now she was deathly white. As she stared across the room her fork clattered to the floor from suddenly nerveless fingers.

"Kerry, what is it?" Mel half rose from her seat because Kerry looked ready to faint but Pierce caught her arm and pulled her down again.

"She'll be all right in a minute. Seeing her father for the first time in three years has given her a bit of a shock." He poured a glass of water and pushed it into Kerry's hand. "Drink this and breath slowly…in…out…in…out. There's a good girl."

Although he was treating her like a child she instinctively obeyed him, concentrating on her breathing while the room whirled around her in a kaleidoscope of color and her ears filled with the echoes of her father's laughter. The others watched anxiously, their conversation floating just out of reach so she saw their lips moving without having the least idea of what they were saying. She could tell Pierce and David were arguing though and for a brief moment she wondered why, and then she began to let go. It would be easier to leave all this confusion behind her. She closed her eyes.

"Kerry! Don't run out on me now sweetheart. This time you're going to face everything and everyone, including that bastard who calls himself your father," Pierce sounded angrier than she'd ever heard him.

It was his anger that did it because deep in the shadows that were clouding her consciousness she suddenly realized he wasn't angry with her at all. His black fury was directed at other people...her father for one, maybe even Marissa. Slowly she opened her eyes and the color began to seep back into her cheeks.

"I'm fine now," she was surprised to find she was clutching Pierce's hand and that she didn't want to let go of it...ever."

"Good, because this is your big moment," he gave her a grim little smile of encouragement before his gaze travelled to a point slightly above and beyond her left shoulder. Instinctively she looked round only to be half blinded by the light of a camera flash.

Indignant waiters rushed to her rescue but they were too late. The grinning photographer already had his picture and as he checked it out on his digital display his smile grew wider. This was one for the papers...a picture of Pierce Simon holding hands with a girl of such delicate beauty she would illuminate the nation's breakfast tables even while readers were trying to discover who she was.

The bright flash had directed all eyes towards their table and within moments Marissa had seen Pierce and was crossing the room trailing her escort like a slightly cumbersome tug.

"Pierce darling, why didn't you tell me you'd be here tonight," she exclaimed, her theatrical approach solely for the benefit of the photographer.

"Possibly because you weren't on my guest list," his answer was terse to the point of rudeness although he couched it in a polite smile as he stood up. "Besides I didn't think your friend would find me the most congenial of company."

Marissa gave a little tinkling laugh. "Don't be silly darling. Charles would love to meet you again after so long."

"Would you Charles? In that case I'll arrange it." Pierce beckoned to one of the waiters and asked him to rearrange the seating while Charles Farrow directed a furious look at Marissa. He didn't notice Kerry until the extra chairs arrived and everyone shuffled up to make room for them. When he did it threw him so totally that she had a sudden glimpse of the old, lonely man he would eventually become when tanning studios and Botox could no longer hide the fact he was getting older. In that moment his usual svelte sophistication, his arrogance, and his cool confidence faded. It was a fleeting image and then he visibly pulled himself together, straightening his spine and tightening his jaw.

"Hello Kerry." His voice was impersonal, his greeting about as warm as a midwinter day.

"Hello Father," she was relieved to find she felt nothing for him. No bitterness. No love. Not even sadness for what might have been. That one brief glimpse into his future was responsible. The lonely, selfish old man who had looked out of his eyes for one unguarded moment had shifted her hold on reality. With a sudden sense of release she knew he no longer mattered. Three years of struggling, of living one day at a time because the future was too bleak to contemplate, had turned her into a different person. Now she was someone whose confidence could no longer be shaken by the man who had never shown her any affection.

Pierce seemed to sense her change of attitude and he squeezed her hand as he nodded to an additional newcomer. It wasn't a humorous smile but it was one that conveyed a good deal of satisfaction. "I had no idea I was so popular. Have you come to join us as well Richard?"

They all looked at the famous gossip columnist with startled surprise, partly because his presence at the table was so unexpected, and partly because his columns were flamboyant, witty and frequently vitriolic and yet he was such an unobtrusive man. He was someone who would never be noticed in a crowd. He gave them a wide smile without a trace of apology.

"Sorry to butt in folks but I'm just doing my job. All I want are a few quotes and then I'll leave you in peace. Celebrating something are you?"

"My birthday," Pierce's eyes sparkled when he saw Charles Farrow's fury. He knew that the older man suspected a set up but also knew he was in no position to prove it.

The journalist pulled a notebook out of an inner pocket as he directed his first question. "No chance of you returning to the tennis circuit then?"

"None! It's a young man's sport." Pierce's fingers tightened on Kerry's although he didn't look at her.

"And you think you're over the hill at thirty-four?" Richard Jennings had obviously done his homework.

This time it was Pierce's turn to smile with what appeared to be genuine amusement. "Not exactly over the hill...just setting out on a different journey. The tennis circuit is great for the young and single and I wouldn't have missed it for the world. It's given me everything I have. Without it I wouldn't be in the position I am today where I can pick and choose what I do."

"But?" With the unerring instinct of a seasoned journalist, the older man sensed a scoop.

"But it's no place for a married man with children." Pierce shrugged, apparently bored by the question.

Richard Jennings glanced quickly at Marissa before he looked back at Pierce. "Do I take it you're about to announce a date?"

"For what?" Pierce gave him the sort of long, cool gaze that would have thrown someone less thick skinned.

"Your engagement of course."

"It's a bit late for that," Pierce threw back his head and laughed. "For once in your life you've been out-gunned Richard. Let me introduce you to my wife Kerry, and to her father, Charles Farrow of Farrow Holdings."

The journalist was momentarily speechless, capable only of gazing at Kerry in open mouthed disbelief. Marissa flushed as red as her vivid dress and gave a tight little gasp of fury as her gaze slid past Pierce to where Kerry was sitting, still holding tightly onto his hand. When she had first arrived at the table she had been so intent on the photographer she had dismissed her as someone of no consequence, not even checking to see who she was. Now, however, she recognized her and her claws came out.

"Why Kerry, how lovely to see you," her smile was totally insincere. "I didn't know it was you because it's been so long, and you look very different without that yard of hair hanging down your back."

Kerry smiled. She knew what she had to do. "The children made it impractical," she explained, joining in with Pierce's game. "You know what they're like when they're tiny...all that grabbing onto everything and pulling hard."

Marissa's blank expression said that not only did she not know what small children were like but she didn't have the faintest clue what Kerry was talking about either. It was left to Richard Jennings to clear everything up.

"Are you telling me you're married and you have a child?" He directed his question at Pierce although his eyes rested on Kerry with considerable admiration, taking in the detail of her clinging pink dress and the sheen of her urchin curls.

"Children," corrected Pierce. "We have twins, Ben and Lauren. They're two years old." The pride in his voice was genuine despite the game he was having at everyone's expense.

With an exclamation of disgust the journalist threw his notebook down amongst the debris of the meal. "I must be in the wrong job. Pierce Simon married with two children and I haven't reported it. For god's sake I'm a gossip columnist. News like this is meant to reach me as it happens."

"Your problem not mine. I didn't ask other people to hit the ball for me when I played tennis," Pierce chuckled as he slipped his arm around Kerry's shoulders and pulled her closer.

He forestalled any more questions by waving over the waiter and asking for extra glasses and a fresh bottle of wine. Then he carried on with the conversation. "Publicity is as bad for a marriage and children as a life on the tennis circuit, so Kerry and I choose to keep a low profile. I guess we've done well to keep it quiet for this long."

If Richard Jennings recognized he'd been maneuvered away from asking about dates and details, he didn't comment. Instead he turned to Charles Farrow.

"And what about you Sir? What do you think about your grandchildren and the elaborate security screen that has kept them out of the public eye for two years? As owner of Farrow Holdings surely you would have liked to acknowledge them in public occasionally, tell the world your daughter and son-in-law are building a Farrow dynasty."

Charles Farrow gave the reporter a long, cold look. "I honored their request for privacy," he said. Not by so much as the flicker of an eyelid did he give away his real feelings.

Richard Jennings probed a little deeper, too old a hand to be put off by a glacial stare. "Then there's no truth in the story that's been circulating for years now, that you and your daughter are estranged?"

"Surely the fact that we're sitting at the same table answers your question."

Because there was no reply to this, the journalist turned, somewhat desperately, to

Marissa. "And what about you Miss Reynolds? You must have been party to this clever ploy to keep reporters at bay. After all you're pretty high profile yourself, so did you do a deal? Those occasional pictures of you and Pierce together, were they a part of it? Were they all about boosting your career while Pierce kept us all looking in totally the wrong direction?"

Marissa managed something fairly close to a smile as she grabbed what little credit she could. "Pierce and I have been friends for years."

Richard Jennings nodded, satisfied he'd put the right two and two together and completely unaware he'd made five. Then a though struck him. He turned again to Pierce.

"Why now? If you've managed to keep the paparazzi fooled all this time, why broadcast now?"

"Who's broadcasting?" Pierce shook his head. "I'm just here for a quiet meal."

"You didn't telephone the paper then?"

"And hand you my privacy on a plate. I'm not mad you know!"

"I'm beginning to think I might be," the journalist gave up on Pierce with a disgruntled frown and turned to David. "You're not planning to retire or anything are you because this seems to be a night for big news?"

David chuckled. "I intend to be sports fodder for a few years yet."

"No wedding bells sounding in your direction then?" He looked at Mel as he spoke but David shook his head.

"None! And before you resort to fantasy let me introduce you to Mel Parker. She manages the Spa Bistro at Greenleas and she is also Mrs Simon's business partner."

Chapter Eleven

Kerry was very quiet on the journey back to Greenleas. She sat well away from Pierce in a tight little world of her own. He didn't speak to her as they covered the few miles between the restaurant and the sports club but she was aware of an enormous tension building between them, a tension that could only be resolved in one way.

He pulled into the car park and killed the engine so they were alone in a pool of darkness. "Are you sure you didn't want to go on to the nightclub with David and Mel?"

"Quite sure," her voice was little more than a whisper as she aimed for humor. "It's all right for them, they don't get woken up at six o'clock every morning."

Sensing his smile, she could picture his rueful expression. Their lives had become so interwoven in the past few weeks that she now knew what to expect from him on most occasions. They were no longer two people linked by an unplanned fusion of genes. Instead they were two people with mutual aims who might learn to be friends. She put out a hand and touched his arm. He was no more than a dark shadow sitting beside her.

"I want to thank you...for tonight," her words were halting as she searched for a way to explain how she felt. She needed him to know that by making her face her father he had exorcised a demon. It no longer mattered that Charles Farrow had let her down at the most crucial moment of her life. After tonight she would be able to view everything more objectively, maybe even see her father's side of the story. Perhaps they could even talk about it at sometime in the future although they hadn't made any plans to meet. She tried to explain all this to Pierce, to talk to him for the first time about the trauma of her early pregnancy.

He listened in silence while she told him how her father had tried to make her have an abortion and how he'd thrown her out of the house when she refused. "And the way he talked about it made everything that had happened between you and me seem dirty somehow...I...I can't really explain...but it was..."

With an exclamation of disgust Pierce pulled her into his arms. "Stop it!" That's nonsense and you know it." His mouth was very close to hers.

She could sense the anger surging through him and for a moment she wasn't sure whether it was directed at her because of what she had just told him about her feelings or whether it was directed at her father. His next action left her in no doubt and when they finally drew apart they were both trembling with the intensity of their need for one another. With a muttered curse Pierce threw open the driver's door. The interior light clicked on, illuminating Kerry's flushed cheeks and the moist redness of her lips.

"We've still got to get rid of George and Mary," he groaned, his eyes blue pools of turbulence that spoke a language of their own as they caressed every inch of her face.

She put out a finger and touched his mouth, tracing the familiar lines of his lips until he gave an anguished moan. "For god's sake Kerry, I can't take much more of this. Three years is a long time to be celibate."

She drew back from him then, a tiny frown of unease on her face. Surely he wasn't going to start lying now, not when everything was beginning to make sense.

"What about Marissa?"

"What about Marissa?" He caught her fingers and kissed each one before turning her hand over and pressing his lips against her palm.

Angrily she curled it into a fist. "Stop playing with me Pierce. You know exactly what I mean and if we're to make anything of our marriage we must at least be truthful with one another."

"You mean there is some chance of success after all?" He was teasing her now, totally confident until he saw the expression in her eyes. He stopped laughing then and shook his head.

"Ah…forgive me sweetheart, and believe me too. You've no reason to be jealous of Marissa."

"Despite the fact I saw you kissing her?"

"Despite the fact you saw her kissing me, as I told you at the time."

"There's a difference?"

"There is most decidedly a difference," he gave a soft chuckle as he lowered his head to the scooped neck of her pink dress. "Would you like me to demonstrate?"

"Not yet," the breathlessness returned to her voice as his lips brushed her throat. "Not until you've explained about Marissa."

He gave a sigh of frustration. "All right, you win. Marissa has been seeing your father on and off for years, ever since she first met him in fact. I think he's her security blanket in case she doesn't land someone closer to her own age."

"Like Pierce Simon?"

"You said it," he gave a twisted grin. "I've had to work hard at keeping her at arm's length these past few years without frightening her off altogether."

When he saw her puzzlement his expression softened. "Strange as it might sound, she was the only contact I had with you. Because of her relationship with your father I kept hoping that if I strung her along she would eventually let something drop, pass on the information I was sure your father was keeping from me. Don't forget I only found out the real truth a few weeks ago. Until then I thought your father was acting on your instructions. I had absolutely no idea he'd thrown you out, still less that you were pregnant. To be fair I don't think Marissa knew either. I'd hazard a guess you weren't one of their regular topics of conversation!"

He paused and dropped a gentle kiss on her upturned face. "Don't look like that Kerry. It's all over now. When you saw me with Marissa I had just told her I was too busy to keep on meeting up with her and she was trying to salvage a little pride by attempting to turn me on."

"Did she succeed?" The corners of Kerry's mouth started to curl upwards.

"What do you think?"

"I'd like you to tell me."

"Well considering I'd just spent a very frustrating night holding you in my arms, I think I was very controlled, especially when Marissa made it clear she was available."

"I was available too," Kerry lowered her head and spoke into his shoulder. "That first night when you carried me into your bed showed me exactly how I felt about you. I was ready to agree to anything until I saw you with Marissa."

He put his hand under her chin and tilted her face upwards again until he could look into her eyes. "What a terrible mess we've made of things Kerry! I don't think either of us have done anything right. I need to know exactly why you ran away from me too. And remember it's your turn to tell the truth now."

She told him, reminding him of the conversation at the bar the day she discovered she was pregnant, and explaining how his insistence that marriage and babies had no place on the tennis circuit stopped her from telling him anything at all. "I didn't want to be responsible for wrecking your career," she explained. "I was the one who was careless, so I thought I had to be responsible, not you."

"You mean you took away any choice on my part even though I was at least fifty per cent to blame, more really because you were barely more than a child yourself, because you thought you had to. I can't believe you were afraid I would behave like your father. I'm sorry Kerry. Sorry you had so little faith in me. Sorry I dragged you round the circuit without at least some promises for the future. Sorry your father was your only role model. Did you really think I would abandon you if I knew you were pregnant?"

"Not abandon me, no. But I thought you might hate me for what I'd done to you and that you'd resent the baby I was expecting the way my father always resented me, and I couldn't face it."

He held her tightly then. "Thank god I found you before you had time to infect Ben and Lauren with all those hang ups. I love you Kerry and I always have. My mistake was not to tell you sooner. I thought making love to you was enough...that there would be plenty of time to talk about getting married later. I was so wrapped up in my career that I didn't think about anything but the next match. It was only when you left me that I realized how much I needed you in my life. Anyway your parent's problems are not ours. The twins belong to both of us whereas you only belonged to your mother."

She stirred in his arms, the vitriol of her father's reaction when she'd first told him she was pregnant returning to her in a rush of puzzled emotion. Pierce looked down at her with a frown. "I'm sorry I'm the one who has to tell you this because it isn't a pretty story. It's the one thing I learned from Marissa though. She let it all out one night when we went for a drink. Apparently your father is infertile but he didn't tell your mother this when he married her. When she found out she understandably became very angry and upset. I imagine it was her anger that drove her into the arms of one of his business partners, a married man many years older than her, and someone who should have known better. Anyway, you were the result, but for some reason your father decided to accept you as his own child. It was probably because Farrow Holdings was the most important thing in his life. If he'd fallen out with his business partner it would have damaged the company and if he'd divorced your mother it would have cost him a lot of money."

"When you were born he even celebrated your arrival by telling journalists you were the new heir to the company. Of course that was his public face. In the privacy of his home he never forgave your mother for what she'd done, or forgave you for being born. You were a constant reminder of her infidelity, his own lack of fertility and the perfidy of his business partner."

Kerry's eyes were twin pools of agony for her parent's dilemma as she stared up at him. "That's why she always taught me I had to accept the consequences of my own mistakes, and it must be why she agreed to send me away to boarding school as well. I know she didn't want to but she probably decided it was better than keeping me at home with a father who resented every breath I took. Her life must have been hell."

"His too I guess," Pierce said. "Because although he agreed to accept you as his own child, he never got over it. Instead he made sure you and your mother suffered as a consequence. According to Marissa he still takes pride in the fact he never let her forget what she'd done, right up to the day she died."

"What a terrible way to live. You're right, it must have been hell for both of them."

"Not as hellish as my life has been for the last three years though." He lifted his arms from her shoulders and cupped her face in his hands. "Do you know exactly what I've been through, searching for you, not knowing what I'd done to make you leave me? And finding you only made it worse. First you tried to put me off with that ridiculous story about being bored with tennis. Deep down I knew it was a lie but until I saw the twins I didn't understand what you were trying to do. Once I realized it was because you were trying to protect yourself and them, it all began to make sense. Then I saw how little faith you had in me and how you were convinced I would always put my own needs first and it made me realize how much I'd failed you."

"Failed me?" Kerry shook her head in disbelief. "How can you say such a thing when I've stolen two years of Ben and Lauren's babyhood from you? I don't know how you can ever forgive me."

"I forgave you the first moment I saw you with them," he kissed her gently. "When I saw how pale and tired you were, how thin you'd become, all I wanted was to take you in my arms and keep you there forever. And when I realized what a terrible struggle you'd had bringing them up all alone, I thought I'd go mad. I was telling the truth when I said I forced you to marry me quickly because I wanted to protect you and the children from any media probing, but I had an ulterior motive too. I didn't trust you not to run away again and I couldn't bear the thought of losing you for a second time, so I just hoped, given time, that you would stop hating me for being such a bully and learn to love me again."

"You mean it wasn't all about Ben and Lauren at all? Are you saying you wouldn't have fought me in court?"

He shook his head. "I couldn't have hurt you that much? No, I'd have supported all three of you and hoped for a second chance if you'd decided to call my bluff. Fortunately for me you didn't."

She smiled then, all the love she'd hidden for so long showing in her eyes. He had always wanted her. It had never just been about the twins.

"But what about this evening?" Her voice was husky with emotion as she turned to him again. "Why play everything out in public? It could all have gone very wrong."

"That's what David said," he frowned as he remembered how his friend had argued with him at the restaurant as soon as he realized what was happening. "He was angry with me for setting everything up but it was a risk I had to take. I knew we couldn't keep our marriage out of the public eye for much longer. A chance remark at Greenleas, someone from the old days recognizing you, and it would be all over the media in a matter of hours. Once I found out where Marissa and your father were eating this evening it was easy. A short anonymous phone call to Richard Jennings, and a quiet word with the waiters, and everything was in place. My plan was to make everyone think we'd been married for a long time. That it also forced your father into a public acknowledgement of our marriage and the twins was a bonus."

"It was cruel to Marissa."

"Marissa is quite capable of taking care of herself. Besides, I found out recently that she is responsible for much of your father's recent bitterness towards you. In the early days of our relationship she fed him stories about you that were totally untrue because she was jealous. I'm not saying he'd have acted any differently to your pregnancy given your history with him but she never gave him the chance to think well of you. Instead she just fuelled his bitterness about your mother's behavior by making out you were free with your sexual favors too."

"How do you know that? Surely Marissa didn't tell you herself."

"Of course not. I telephoned your father a couple of days before we got married because I wanted to put the record straight."

"Why?"

"I felt guilty. By then I knew he'd thrown you out but I was so sure it was all my fault that I had some grand notion of effecting a reunion. Needless to say your father didn't play ball although he did let a few skeletons out of the family closet during our stormy telephone conversation, including all the things Marissa had told him. He didn't even ask why I was phoning him. I guess he just thought I was still looking for you. So in the end I didn't tell him you were back in my life or that we were getting married. I didn't tell Marissa either. By then I'd got the measure of both of them and I didn't want either of them upsetting you."

She slipped her arms around his neck and rested her forehead against his cheek, at last understanding most of his recent behavior. "And I thought you hated me for destroying your plans. I thought you wanted Marissa in your life and that I had spoiled everything for you. It's why I wouldn't let you make love to me. I couldn't bear the thought of sharing you."

He buried his face in her hair and groaned. "Sharing me! My god, what books have you been reading Kerry? You have no idea what I was going through; how difficult it was to look as if I didn't care, particularly when I woke up this morning and discovered you and the children were missing. I went to hell and back in the few minutes I was alone before you returned with my birthday presents."

She remembered his dark despair with shame. All that love and need had been for her after all and she hadn't understood. In fact she had never really understood him at all because she'd always been too full of her own hang ups, too insecure to believe anyone could love her just for herself.

"I'm sorry. I didn't mean to make you so unhappy," she whispered the words into his neck as he held her tightly.

"I'm sorry too," his breath was warm against her cheek as he ducked his head downwards, searching for her mouth. "If I'd given you more of myself at the beginning of

215

our relationship then none of this would have happened. You'd have known how much I loved you and never run away."

With an effort she resisted his kiss as she asked her final question. "And you really can live without tennis?"

He caught her bottom lip between his teeth as he replied. "I've already done so for two years, so why should finding you make a difference?"

"Because you said you left the circuit to look for me."

"So I did," he ran his tongue along the inside of her mouth, sending a quiver of anticipation down her spine. "It was why I bought Greenleas too. I thought if I lived close to your father then one day I might see you again. But none of that is the entire truth. The thing is, without you everything lost its sparkle. When every tennis match became just another slog and every tournament just another meaningless journey, I knew my sporting days were over. I'd hit too many balls in too many places for too long and it was time to get out. I even hoped I might hear from you when I announced my retirement. I wanted to let you know how I felt about you and how your disappearance had made me grow up to the things that really mattered in my life."

She gave a sad little sigh. "And all the time I was living without a television or a computer. I didn't even have time to read a newspaper, so the news about your retirement never filtered through."

He continued to drop butterfly kisses onto her lips. "So much for modern technology. Next time I'll use a carrier pigeon."

She opened her mouth to protest. "There won't be a next time. This is the only double fault we're allowed."

He chuckled as he caught her tongue between his teeth and guided it into his mouth. "It's the only one we need. We're not going to make the same mistake twice."

Chapter Twelve

Much later, with Mary and George dispatched after a cup of coffee that seemed to take an eternity, they faced one another again but this time the width of the sitting room was between them. Nervously Kerry began to collect the dirty mugs. Pierce's hand on her arm made her jump.

"Leave them until tomorrow," he said as he removed a mug from her hand and gently turned her around to face him. "I can think of something much better to do than clear up the sitting room."

"Can you?" she began to tremble as his hand slipped across her back to the zipper on her dress.

"Mmm, and so can you," the nylon clasp snaked downwards taking the dress with it and leaving her neck and shoulders bare. Deliberately he pushed the straps of her lacy bra aside and began a slow assault on her senses, his lips whispering across her skin while his hands dealt deftly with the rest of her clothes. Then he picked her up and carried her through to the bedroom, pausing only long enough to lock the door behind him.

"That will take care of tiny unexpected visitors," he smiled against her mouth "My children are going to have to learn to share you."

She flicked her tongue erotically against his teeth and felt his body tense on an indrawn breath as he lowered her onto the bed. A wild exultation raced through her as she realized how much power she had. He saw the knowledge in her eyes and smiled as he started to unfasten the buttons of his shirt with shaking fingers.

"Don't ever doubt it again my darling. I couldn't bear to lose you twice."

She knelt up on the bed and finished unbuttoning his shirt. Then she loosened his belt and helped him with the rest of his clothes, stroking the muscular contours of his body with the same three-year hunger that soon had him covering every inch of her skin with kisses.

She melted into his embrace with a sigh, her fingers tangling in his hair as he gathered her up into his arms and began to kiss her all over again, slowly at first and then with a wild savagery as he slowly lost control and drowned them both in a passion that said far more than words. Finally he lifted her over onto her back and she welcomed the crushing weight of his body as his chest grazed her swollen nipples. When he saw her little secret smile and he paused and looked down at her, poised agonizingly on the brink of consummation.

"You really have been celibate for three years haven't you?" she said. Her smile widened and then became part of his kiss as he took them both to forgotten heights. And just before they got there he murmured his answer into her mouth with all the love she was ever going to need.

"Angel, you'd better believe it!"

Sheila Claydon books published by BWL Publishing Inc.

Cabin Fever
Reluctant Date
Double Fault
Kissing Maggie Silver
Mending Jodie's Heart (When Paths Meet Book 1)
Finding Bella Blue (When Paths Meet Book 2)
Saving Katy Gray (When Paths Meet Book 3)
Miss Locatelli
Remembering Rose (Mapleby Memories Book 1)
The Sheila Claydon Special Edition
The Hollywood Collection

In the 1980s Sheila Claydon wrote a number of romances under the pseudonym Anne Beverley. Then a busy career and family life got in the way and before she knew it, she had turned her back on the characters who were begging to be liberated from her imagination. Now she is back to writing fiction again and, considerably older and no longer shy, writes under her own name.

Her motto is a quote by the late Ray Bradbury: "First, find out what your hero wants. Then just follow him."

Although family remains central to her life, she still finds the time to read, to write, and to travel. Many of the places she has visited feature in her books. Her fans say that reading them is like buying a ticket to romance.

You can find her at https://www.facebook.com/SheilaClaydon.author/